Franklin K. Young

Chess Generalship

Outlook

Franklin K. Young

Chess Generalship

1. Auflage | ISBN: 978-3-73262-042-5

Erscheinungsort: Frankfurt am Main, Deutschland

Erscheinungsjahr: 2018

Outlook Verlag GmbH, Frankfurt.

Franklin K. Young

Chess Generalship

Outlook

CHESS GENERALSHIP

BY

FRANKLIN K. YOUNG

Vol. I.
GRAND RECONNAISSANCE.

"He who first devised chessplay, made a model of the Art Militarie, representing therein all the concurrents and contemplations of War, without omitting any."

"Examen de Ingenios."

Juan Huarte, 1616.

"Chess is the deepest of all games; it is constructed to carry out the principal of a battle, and the whole theory of Chess lies in that form of action."

Emanuel Lasker.

BOSTON
INTERNATIONAL PUBLISHING CO.
1910

"Chess is the gymnasium for the mind—it does for the brain what athletics does for the body."

Henry Thomas Buckle.

GEORGE E. CROSBY CO., PRINTERS, BOSTON, MASS.

YOUNG'S CHESS WORKS

"There are secrets that the children

Are not taught in public school;

If these secrets were broadcasted,

How could we the masses rule?

If they understood Religion,

Jurisprudence, Trade and War,

Would they groan and sweat and labor—

Make our bricks and furnish straw?"

Anon.

TO

The Memory

OF

EPAMINONDAS
THE INVENTOR
OF
SCIENTIFIC WARFARE

"I leave no sons

To perpetuate my name;

But I leave two daughters—

LEUCTRA and MANTINEA

Who will transmit my fame

To remotest posterity."

"For empire and greatness it importeth most that a people do profess arms as their principal honor, study and occupation."—*Sir Francis Bacon.*

"There is nothing truly imposing but Military Glory."—*Napoleon.*

"The conquered in war, sinking beneath the tribute exacted by the victor and not daring to utter their impotent hatred, bequeath to their children miseries so extreme that the aged have not further evil to fear in death, nor the youthful any good to hope in life."—*Xenocles.*

"War is an element established by the Deity in the order of the World; perpetual peace upon this Earth we inhabit is a dream."—*Von Moltke.*

PREFACE

"To become a good General one well may begin by playing at Chess."—Prince de Condé.

Except the theatre of actual Warfare, no spot known to man furnishes such facilities for the practice of combined strategy, tactics and logistics as does the surface of the Chess-board.

To those familiar with the Science of Strategetics, it needs no proof that ability to play a good game at Chess, indicates the possession of faculties common to all great military commanders.

At a certain point, the talent of Morphy for Chess-play and the talent of Napoleon for Warfare become merged; and beyond this point, their methods of thought and of action are identical.

Opportunity to display, and in most spectacular fashion, their singular and superlative genius, was not wanting to either.

But unlike the ferocious Corsican, whose "only desire is to find myself on the battlefield," the greatest of all Masters at Chess, found in the slaughter of his fellow-creatures no incentive sufficient to call forth those unsurpassed strategetical powers, which recorded Chess-play shows he possessed.

From this sameness of talent, common to the great Chess-player and the great military commander, arises the practical utility of the Royal Game.

For by means of Chess-play, one may learn and practice in their highest interpretation, mental and physical processes of paramount importance to the community in time of extreme peril.

From such considerations and for the further reason that in a true Republic all avenues to greatness are open to merit, scientific Chess-play should be intelligently and systematically taught in the public schools. "A people desirous of liberty will entrust its defense to none but themselves," says the Roman maxim, and in crises, woe to that land where the ruler is but a child in arms, and where the disinclination of the people towards its exercise is equalled by their unfamiliarity with the military habit.

Despite the ethics of civilization, the optimism of the "unco guid" and the unction even of our own heart's deep desire, there seems no doubt but that each generation will have its wars.

"*Pax perpetua*," writes Leibnitz, "exists only in God's acre." Here on earth, if seems that men forever will continue to murder one another for various reasons; all of which, in the future as in the past, will be good and sufficient to the fellow who wins; and this by processes differing only in neatness and despatch.

Whether this condition is commendable or not, depends upon the point of view. Being irremediable, such phase of the subject hardly is worth discussing. However, the following by a well-qualified observer, is interesting and undeniably an intelligent opinion, viz.:

From the essay on "WAR," read by Prof. John Ruskin at Woolwich, (Eng.) Military Academy.

"All the pure and noble arts of Peace are founded on War; no great Art ever rose on Earth, but among a nation of soldiers.

"As Peace is established or extended the Arts decline. They reach an unparalleled pitch of costliness, but lose their life, enlist themselves at last on the side of luxury and corruption and among wholly tranquil nations, wither utterly away.

"So when I tell you that War is the foundation of all the Arts, I mean also that it is the foundation of all the high virtues and faculties of men.

"It was very strange for me to discover this and very dreadful—but I saw it to be quite an undeniable fact.

"We talk of Peace and Learning, of Peace and Plenty, of Peace and Civilization; but I found that those were not the words which the Muse of History coupled together; but that on her lips the words were—Peace and Selfishness, Peace and Sensuality, Peace and Corruption, Peace and Death.

"I found in brief, that all great nations learned their truth of word and strength of thought in War; that they were nourished in War and wasted in Peace; taught by War and deceived by Peace; trained by War and betrayed by Peace; that they were born in War and expired in Peace.

"Creative, or foundational War, is that in which the natural restlessness and love of contest among men, is disciplined into modes of beautiful—though it may be fatal—play; in which the natural ambition and love of Power is chastened into aggressive conquest of surrounding evil; and in which the natural instincts of self-defence are sanctified by the nobleness of the institutions which they are appointed to defend.

"For such War as this all men are born; in such War as this any man may happily die; and forth from such War as this have arisen throughout the Ages, all the highest sanctities and virtues of Humanity."

———————

That our own country may escape the common lot of nations, is something not even to be hoped.

Defended by four almost bottomless ditches, nevertheless it is a certainty that coming generations of Americans must stand in arms, not only to repel foreign aggression, but to uphold even the integrity of the Great Republic; and with the hand-writing of coming events flaming on the wall, posterity well may heed the solemn warning of by-gone centuries:

"As man is superior to the brute, so is a trained and educated soldier superior to the merely brave, numerous and enthusiastic."

———————

"The evils to be apprehended from a standing army are remote and in my judgment, not to be dreaded; but the consequence of lacking one is inevitable ruin."—Washington.

———————

CONTENTS

"The progress of Science universally is retarded, because sufficient attention is not paid to explaining essentials in particular and exactly to define the terms employed."—Euclid.

"The first care of the sage should be to discover the true character of his pupils. By his questions he should assist them to explain their own ideas and by his answers he should compel them to perceive their falsities. By accurate definitions he should gradually dispel the incongruities in their earlier education and by his subtlety in arousing their doubts, he should redouble their curiosity and eagerness for information; for the art of the instructor consists in inciting his pupils to that point at which they cannot endure their manifest ignorance.

"Many, unable to undergo this trial and confounded by offended self-conceit and lacking the fortitude to sustain correction, forsake their master, who should not be eager to recall them. Others who learn from humiliation to distrust themselves should no longer have snares spread for their vanity. The master should speak to them neither with the severity of a censor nor with the haughtiness of a sophist, nor deal in harsh reproaches nor importunate complaints; his discourse should be the language of reason and friendship in the mouth of experience."—Socrates.

INTRODUCTORY

"The test is as true of cerebral power, as if a hundred thousand men lay dead upon the field; or a score of hulks were swinging blackened wrecks, after a game between two mighty admirals."—Dr. Oliver Wendell Holmes.

(Opening Address at Morphy Banquet, Boston, 1859.)

———————

Men whose business it is to understand war and warfare often are amused by senseless comparisons made by writers who, as their writings show, are ignorant even of the rudiments of military art and science. Of course a certain license in expression of thought is not to be denied the layman; he cannot be expected to talk with the exactness of the man who knows. At the same time there is a limit beyond which the non-technical man passes at his peril, and this limit is reached when he poses as a critic and presumes to dogmatize on matters in regard to which he is uninformed.

The fanciful conjectures of such people, well are illustrated by the following editorial *faux pas*, perpetrated by a leading metropolitan daily, viz.:

"Everyone knows now that a future war between states having similar and substantially equal equipments will be a different affair from any war of the past; characterized by a different order of generalship and a radically novel application of the principles of strategy and tactics."

Many in the struggle to obtain their daily bread, are tempted to essay the unfamiliar, and for a stipulated wage to pose as teachers to the public.

Such always will do well to write modestly in regard to sciences which they have not studied and of arts which they never practiced, and especially in future comments on Military matters, such people may profit by the appended modicum of that ancient history, which newspaper men as a class so affect to despise, and in regard to which, as a rule, they are universally and lamentably, ignorant.

What orders of Generalship can exist in the future, different from those which always have existed since war was made, viz.: good generalship and bad generalship?

Ability properly to conduct an army is a concrete thing; it does not admit of comparison. Says Frederic the Great:

"There are only two kinds of Generals—those who know their trade and those who do not."

Hence, "a different order of Generalship," suggested by the editorial quoted, implies either a higher or a lesser degree of ability in the "general of the future"; and as obviously, it is impossible that he can do worse than many already have done, it is necessary to assume that the commander of tomorrow will be an improvement over his predecessors.

Consequently, to the military mind it becomes of paramount interest to inquire as to the form and manner in which such superiority will be tangibly and visibly manifested, viz.:

Will the general of the future be a better general than Epaminondas, Alexander, Hannibal, Caesar, Gustavus Adolphus, Turenne, Eugene, Frederic, Washington, Napoleon, Von Moltke?

Will he improve upon that application of the principles of strategy and tactics to actual warfare which comes down to us of today, stamped with the approval of these superlative military geniuses?

Will the general of the future know a better way for making war than acting against the enemy's communications?

Will he devise a better method of warfare than that whose motive is the concentration of a superior force upon the strategetic objective?

Will the processes of his prime logistic operations be preferable to those of men who won their victories before their battles were fought, by combining with their troops the topography of the country, and causing rivers and mountains to take the place of corps d'armee?

Will the general of the future renounce as obsolete and worthless that military organization founded centuries before the Christian Era, by the great Theban, Epaminondas, the father of scientific warfare; that system adopted by every captain of renown and which may be seen in its purity in the greater military establishments from the days of Rome to the present Imperial North German Confederation?

Will the general of the future renounce as obsolete and worthless that system of Minor Tactics utilized by every man who has made it his business to conquer the World? Will he propose to us something more perfect than the primary formation of forces depicted in Plate XIII of the Secret Strategical Instructions of Frederic II?

Will the general of the future renounce as obsolete and worthless those intricate, but mathematically exact, evolutions of the combined arms, which appertain to the Major Tactics of men who are remembered to this day for the battles that they won?

Will he invent processes more destructive than those whereby Epaminondas crushed at Leuctra and Mantinea the power of Sparta, and the women of Lacedaemon saw the smoke of an enemy's camp fire for the first time in six hundred years?

Than those whereby Alexander, a youth of eighteen, won Greece for his father at Chaeronea and the World for himself at Issus and Arbela? Than those whereby Hannibal destroyed seriatim four Roman armies at Trebia, Thrasymenus, Cannae and Herdonea?

Will he find out processes more sudden and decisive than those whereby Caesar conquered Gaul and Pompey and the son of Mithridates, and which are fitly described only in his own language; "Veni, vidi, vici"?

What will the general of the future substitute for the three contiguous sides of the octagon whereby Tamerlane the Great with his 1,400,000 veterans at the Plains of Angora, enveloped the Emperor Bajazet and 900,000 Turks in the most gigantic battle of record?

Will he eclipse the pursuit of these latter by Mizra, the son of Tamerlane, who with the Hunnish light cavalry rode two hundred and thirty miles in five days and captured the Turkish capital, the Emperor Bajazet, his harem and the royal treasure?

Will he excel Gustavus Adolphus, who dominated Europe for twenty years, and Turenne, the military Atlas who upheld that magnificent civilization which embellishes the reign of Louis XIV?

Will he do better than Prince Eugene, who victoriously concluded eighteen campaigns and drove the Turks out of Christendom?

Will he discover processes superior to those whereby Frederic the Great with 22,000 troops destroyed at Rosbach a French army of 60,000 regulars in an hour and a half, at the cost of three hundred men; and at Leuthern with 33,000 troops, killed, wounded or captured 54,000 out of 93,000 Austrians, at a cost of 3,900 men?

Will he improve on those processes whereby Napoleon with 40,000 men, destroyed in a single year five Austrian armies and captured 150,000 prisoners? Will he improve on Rivoli, Austerlitz, Jena, Friedland, Wagram, Dresden, and Ligny?

Will the general of the future renounce as obsolete and worthless that system of Grand Tactics, by means of which the mighty ones of Earth have swept before them all created things?

Will his system surpass in grandeur of conception and exactness of execution the march of Alexander to the Indus? Will he reply to his rival's prayers for peace and amity as did the great Macedonian; "There can be but one Master of the World"; and to the dissuasions of his friend; "So would I do, were I Parmenio"?

Will he do things more gigantic than Hannibal's march across the Alps?

Than the operation of Alesia by Caesar; where the Romans besieging one Gallic army in a fortified city, and themselves surrounded by a second Gallic army, single handed destroyed both? Than the circuit of the Caspian Sea by the 200,000 light cavalry of Tamerlane, a feat of mountain climbing which never has been duplicated? Than that marvelous combination of the principles of tactics and of field fortification, whereby in the position of Bunzelwitz, Frederic the Great, with 55,000 men, successfully upheld the last remaining prop of the Prussian nation, against 250,000 Russian and Austrian regular troops, commanded by the best generals of the age?

Will he conceive anything more scientific and artistic than the manoeuvre of Trenton and Princeton by Washington? Than the capture of Burgoyne at Saratoga and Cornwallis at Yorktown? Than the manoeuvres of Ulm, of Jena, of Landshut? Than the manoeuvres of Napoleon in 1814? Than the manoeuvre of Charleroi in 1815, declared by Jomini to be Napoleon's masterpiece? Will he excel the manoeuvres of Kutosof and Wittsengen in 1812-13 and of Blucher on Paris in 1814 and on Waterloo in 1815; each of which annihilated for the time being the military power of France?

Will he devise military conceptions superior to those whereby Von Moltke overthrew Denmark in six hours, Austria in six days, and France in six weeks?

———————

The sapient race of quill-drivers ever has hugged to its breast many delusions; some of which border upon the outer intellectual darkness. One of these delusions is that most persistently advertised, least substantial, but forever darling first favorite of timid and inexperienced minds: *"The pen is mightier than the sword."*

Explanation of the invincible ignorance of the penny-a-liner is simple, viz.:

Of the myriad self-appointed educators to the public, few are familiar even with the rudimentary principles of Military Science and almost none are acquainted even with the simplest processes of Strategetic Art. Hence, like all who discourse on matters which they do not understand, such writers continually confound together things which have no connection.

Ignorant of war and the use of weapons; bewildered by the prodigious improvements in mechanical details, they immoderately magnify the importance of such improvements, oblivious to the fact that these latter relate exclusively to elementary tactics and in no way affect the system of Strategy, Logistics, and the higher branches of Tactics.

Of such people, the least that can be said and that in all charity, is, that before essaying the role of the pedagogue, they should endeavor to grasp that most obvious of all truths:

"A man cannot teach what he never has learned."

Says Frederic the Great: "Improvements and new discoveries in implements of warfare will be made continually; and generals then alive must modify tactics to comply with these novelties. But the Grand Art of taking advantage of topographical conditions and of the faulty disposition of the opposing forces, ETERNALLY WILL REMAIN UNCHANGED in the military system."

Naturally, the student now is led to inquire:

What then is this immutable military system? What are its text books, where is it taught and from whom is it to be learned?

In answer it may be stated:

At the present day, private military schools make no attempt to teach more than elementary tactics. Even the Governmental academy curriculum aims little higher than the school of the battalion.

Scientific Chess-play begins where these institutions leave off, and ends at that goal which none of these institutions even attempt to reach.

Chess teaches to conduct campaigns, to win battles, and to move troops securely and effectively in the presence of and despite the opposition of an equal or superior enemy.

Military schools graduate boys as second-lieutenants commanding a platoon. Chess graduates Generals, able to mobilize Corps d'armee, whatever their number or location; to develop these into properly posted integers of a grand Strategic Front and to manoeuvre and operate the army as a Strategetic Unit, in accordance to the laws of the Strategetic art and the principles of the Strategetic science.

By precept and by actual practice, Chess teaches what is *NOT* taught in any military school—that least understood and most misunderstood; that best guarded and most invaluable of all State Secrets—

The profession of

GENERALSHIP.

"Books will speak plain when counsellors blanch. Therefore it is good to be conversant with them; especially the books of such as themselves have been actors upon the stage."—Sir Francis Bacon.

"At this moment, Europe, which fears neither God nor devil, grovels in terror before a little man hardly five feet in height; who, clad in a cocked hat and grey great-coat and mounted upon a white horse, plods along through mud and darkness; followed by the most enthusiastic, most devoted and most efficient band of cut-throats and robbers, the world has ever seen."

"Many good soldiers are but poor generals."—Hannibal.

"No soldier serving under a victorious commander, ever has enough of war."—Caesar.

"Officers always should be chosen from the nobility and never from the lower orders of society; for the former, no matter how dissolute, always retain a sense of honor, while the latter, though guilty of atrocious actions, return to their homes without compunction and are received by their families without disapprobation."—Frederic the Great.

At the terrible disaster of Cannae, the Patrician Consul Aemilius Paulus and 80,000 Romans died fighting sword in hand; while the Plebian Consul, Varro, fled early in the battle. Upon the return of the latter to Rome, the Senate, instead of ordering his execution, with withering sarcasm formally voted him its thanks and the thanks of the Roman people, "that he did not despair of the Republic."

"Among us we have a man of singular character—one Phocion. He

14

seems not to know that he lives in our modern age and at incomparable Athens. He is poor, yet is not humiliated by his poverty; he does good, yet never boasts of it; and gives advice, though he is certain it will not be followed. He possesses talent without ambition and serves the state without regard to his own interest. At the head of the army, he contents himself with restoring discipline and beating the enemy. When addressing the assembly, he is equally unmoved by the disapprobation or the applause of the multitude.

"We laugh at his singularities and we have discovered an admirable secret for revenging ourselves for his contempt. He is the only general we have left—but we do not employ him; he is the most upright and perhaps the most intelligent of our counsellors—but we do not listen to him. It is true, we cannot make him change his principles, but, by Heaven, neither shall he induce us to change ours; and it never shall be said that by the example of his superannuated virtues and the influence of his antique teachings, Phocion was able to correct the most polished and amiable people in the world."— Callimedon.

GENERALSHIP

CHESS GENERALSHIP

"In Chess the soldiers are the men and the General is the mind of the player."—Emanuel Lasker.

"It is neither riches nor armies that make a nation formidable; but the courage and genius of the Commander-in-Chief."—Frederic the Great.

"Ho! Ye Macedonians! Because together we have conquered the World, think ye to give law to the blood of Achilles and to withstand the dictates of the Son of Jupiter?

"Choose ye a new commander, draw yourselves up for battle; I will lead against you those Persians whom ye so despise, and if you are victorious, by Mehercule, I will do everything that you desire."— Alexander the Great.

"It is I and I alone, who give you your glory and your success."— Napoleon.

"My thoughts are not your thoughts, neither are your ways, My ways, saith the Lord."—Holy Bible.

By authority indisputable, the ex-cathedra dictum of the greatest of the Great Captains, we have been informed that the higher processes of the military system, eternally will remain unchanged.

As a necessary corollary, it follows that these processes always have been and always will be comprehended and employed by every great Captain.

Equally, it is self-evident, that capability to comprehend these higher processes, united with ability properly to utilize them to win battles and campaigns, constitutes genius for Warfare.

Moreover, we are further informed by the same unimpeachable authority, that so irresistible is genius for warfare, that united to courage, it is formidable beyond the united financial and military resources of the State. In corroboration of this, we have the testimony of well-qualified judges. Says the Count de Saxe:

"Unless a man is born with talent for war and this talent is brought to perfection, it is impossible for him to be more than an indifferent general."

———————

In these days, more or less degenerate from the soldierly standpoint, the fantastic sophistries of Helvetius have vogue, and most people believe book-learning to be all-in-all.

Many are so weak-minded, as really to believe, that because born in the Twentieth Century, they necessarily are the repository of all the virtues, and particularly of all the knowledge acquired by their ancestors from remotest generations. Few seem to understand that the child, even of ultra-modern conditions, is born just as ignorant and often invincibly so, as were the sons of Ham, Shem and Japhet, and most appear to be unaware, that:

Only by intelligent reflection upon their own experience and upon the experiences of others, can one acquire knowledge.

The triviality of crowding the memory with things that may or may not be true, is the merest mimicry of education.

Real education is nothing more than the fruit of experience; and he who acts in conformity to such knowledge, alone is wise. Thus to act, implies ability to comprehend. But there are those in whom capability is limited; hence, all may not be wise who wish to be so, and these necessarily remain through life very much as they are born.

The use of knowledge would be infinitely more certain, if our understanding of its accurate application were as extensive as our needs require. We have only a few ideas of the attributes of matter and of the laws of mechanics, out of an infinite number of secrets which mankind never can hope to discover. This renders our feeble adaptations in practice of the knowledge we possess, oftimes inadequate for the result we desire; and it seems obvious that if Nature had intended man to attain to the superlative, she would have endowed him with intelligence and have communicated to him information, infinitely superior to that we possess.

The universal blunder of mankind arises from an hallucination that all minds are created equal; and that by mere book-learning, *i.e.*, simply by memorizing what somebody says are facts it is possible for any man to attain to superior and even to superlative ability.

———————

Such profoundly, but utterly mis-educated people, not unnaturally may inquire, by what right speaks the eminent warrior previously quoted. These properly may be informed in the words of Frederic the Great:

"The Count de Saxe is the hero of the bravest action ever done by man." viz.,

A great battle was raging.

Within a magnificent Pavilion in the centre of the French camp, the King, the nobility and the high Ecclesiastics of the realm were grouped about a plain iron cot.

Prone upon this cot, wasted by disease, lay the Count de Saxe, in that stupor which often precedes and usually presages dissolution.

The last rites of the Church had been administered, and the assemblage in silence and apprehension, awaited the approach of a victorious enemy and the final gasp of a general who had never lost a battle.

The din of strife drawing nearer, penetrated the coma which enshrouded the soul of the great Field-Marshal.

Saxe opened his eyes. His experienced ear told him that his army, routed and disordered, was flying before an exultant enemy.

The giant whose pastime it was to tear horseshoes in twain with his bare hands and to twist nails into corkscrews with his fingers, staggered to his feet, hoarsely articulating fierce and mandatory ejaculations.

Hastily clothed, the Count de Saxe was placed in a litter and borne out of his pavilion into that chaos of ruin and carnage which invariably accompanies a lost battle. Around him, behind and in front, swarmed his broken battalions and disorganized squadrons; while in pursuit advanced majestically in solid column, the triumphant English.

Saxe demanded his horse and armor.

Clad in iron and supported in the saddle on either hand, this modern Achilles galloped to the front of his army; then, at the head of the Scotch Guards, the Irish Brigade, and French Household troops, Saxe in person, led that series of terrific hand-to-hand onslaughts which drove the English army from the field of battle, and gained the famous victory of Fontenoy.

"Furthermore," declares this illustrious Generalissimo of Louis XIV;

"It is possible to make war without trusting anything to accident; this is the highest point of skill and perfection within the province of a general."

"Most men," writes Vergetius, "imagine that strength and courage are sufficient to secure victory. Such are ignorant that when they exist, stratagem vanquishes strength and skill overcomes courage."

In his celebrated work, *Institutorum Rei Militaris*, that source from whence all writers derive their best knowledge of the military methods of the ancients; and by means of which, he strove to revive in his degenerate countrymen that intelligent valor which distinguishes their great ancestors—the famous Roman reiterates this solemn warning:

"Victory in war depends not on numbers, nor on courage; skill and discipline only, can ensure it."

The emphasis thus laid by these great warriors on genius for warfare is still further accentuated by men whose dicta few will dispute, viz.,

"The understanding of the Commander," says Frederic the Great, "has more influence on the outcome of the battle or campaign, than has the prowess of his troops."

Says Napoleon:

"The general is the head, the whole of an army. It was not the Roman army that subjugated Gaul, it was Caesar; nor was it the Carthagenian army that made the Republic tremble to the gates of Rome, it was Hannibal; it was not the Macedonian army which reached the Indus, it was Alexander; it was not the French army which carried war to the Weser and the Inn, it was Turenne; it was not the Prussian army which for seven years defended Prussia against the three strongest powers of Europe, it was Frederic the Great."

From such opinions by men whose careers evince superlative knowledge of the subject, it is clear, that:

I. *There exists a system of Strategetics common to all great commanders;*

II. *That understanding of this system is shown by the skillful use of it;*

III. *That such skill is derived from innate capability;*

IV. *That those endowed by Nature with this talent, must bring their gifts to perfection, by intelligent study.*

So abstruse are the processes of this greatest of all professions, that comprehension of it has been evidenced by eleven men only, viz.:

Epaminondas, Alexander, Caesar, Hannibal, Gustavus Adolphus, Turenne, Eugene, Frederic, Washington, Napoleon, Von Moltke.

Comprehension of this system can be attained, only by innate capability brought to perfection by intelligent study of the words and achievements of these great Captains.

For life is so short and our memories in general so defective, that we ought to seek instruction only from the purest sources.

None but men endowed by Nature with the military mind and trained in the school of the great Captains, are able to write intelligently on the acts and motives of generals of the first order. All the writings of mere literati relative to these uncommon men, no matter how excellent such authors may be, never can rise to anything more than elegant phraseology.

It is of enlightened critics, such as the former, that the youthful student always is first in need. Such will guide him along a road, in which he who has no conductor may easily lose himself. They will correct his blunders considerately, recollecting that should these be ridiculed or treated with severity, talent might be stifled which might hereafter bloom to perfection.

It is a difficult matter to form the average student, and to impart to him that degree of intelligent audacity and confident prudence which is requisite for the proper practice of the Art of Strategetics.

To secure proficiency, the student from the beginning must cheerfully submit himself to a mental discipline, which properly may be termed severe; in order to make his faculties obedient to his will.

Secondly, he must regularly exercise these faculties, in order to make them active and to acquire the habit of implicitly conforming to the laws of the Art; to make himself familiar with its processes, and to establish in his mind that confidence in its practice which can come only through experience.

The student daily should exercise his mind in the routine of deployments, developments, evolutions, manoeuvres, and operations, both on the offensive and on the defensive. These exercises should be imprinted on the memory by closely reviewing the lesson of the previous day.

Even with all this severe and constant effort, time is necessary for practical tactics to become habitual; for the student must become so familiar with these movements and formations that he can execute them instantly and with precision.

To acquire this degree of perfection, much study is necessary; it is a mistake to think otherwise. But this study is its own sufficient reward, for the student soon will find that it has extended his ideas, and *that he is beginning to think in the GREAT.*

At the same time the student should thoroughly instruct himself in military history, topography, logic, mathematics, and the science of fortification. With all of these the strategist must be familiar.

But his chief aim must be to perfect his judgment and to bring it to the highest degree of broadness and exactness.

This is best done by contemplation of the works of the Great Masters.

The past history of Chess-play, is the true school for those who aspire to precedence in the Royal Game. It is their first duty to inform themselves of the processes of the great in every age, in order to shun their errors and to avail of their methods.

It is essential to grasp that system of play common to the Masters; to pursue it step by step. Particularly is it necessary to learn that he who can best deduce consequences in situations whose outcome is in doubt, is the competitor who will carry off the prize from others who act less rationally than himself.

Especially, should the student be wary in regard to what is termed chess analysis, as applied to the so-called "openings" and to the mid-game. Most chess analysts are compilers of falsities occasionally interspersed with truth. Among the prodigious number of variations which they pretend to establish or refute, none may be implicitly relied on in actual play; few are of value except for merely elementary purposes, and many are fallacies fatal to the user.

The reason for this is: whenever men invited by curiosity, seek to examine circumstantially even the less intricate situations on the Chess-board, they at once become lost in a labyrinth abounding in obscurities and contradictions. Those, who ignorant of the synthetic method of calculation, are compelled to depend upon their analytic powers, quickly find that these, on account of the number of unknown quantities, are utterly inadequate.

Any attempt to calculate the true move in Chess-play by analysis, other than in situations devoid of unknown quantities, is futile.

Yet it is of such folly that the mediocre mind is most enamoured. Content with seeing much, it is oblivious to what it cannot see; and the analytical system consists merely in claiming that there is nothing to see, other than what it does see.

This is that slender reed upon which the so-called "chess-analyst" hangs his claims, oblivious to the basic truth that in analysis, unless all is known, nothing is known.

Many delude themselves to the contrary and strive to arrive at correct conclusions without first having arranged clearly before their minds all the facts.

Hence, their opinions and judgments, being founded in ignorance of all the facts, are to that extent defective; and their conclusions necessarily wrong.

Through action taken upon incomplete knowledge, men are beguiled into error; and it is to such unreason that most human catastrophes are to be attributed.

————————

Most of those who attempt to write on Strategetics, and whether applied to Chess-play or to Warfare, very quickly are compelled to seek refuge in vague phrases; in order to conceal their uncertain grasp on the subject discussed.

The uninformed believe in them, because of their reputation, and are satisfied that the thing is so, without understanding *WHY*.

Words intended to convey instruction, should not be used except in their proper meaning. Each word should be defined for the student and its use regulated. The true use of words being established, there is no longer danger from a play upon them; or, from different and confused ideas annexed to them, either by the persons who read, or who employ them.

By means of this warning, the student easily may detect the empty mouthings of enthusiastic inexperience, and equally so, the casuistries of the subtle expert; who often uses language merely to conceal from youthful talent, knowledge which if imparted, might be fatal to his domination.

As the student progresses toward proficiency, he, sooner or later, will come to realize, that of all disgusting things, to a mind which revolts at nonsense, reasoning ill is the worst.

It is distressing, to be afflicted with the absurdities of men, who, victims of the fancy, confound enthusiasm with capability and mistake mania for talent. The world is full of such people, who, in all honesty thinking themselves philosophers, are only visionaries enamoured of their own lunatic illusions.

The true discipline for the student who aspires to proficiency at Chess-play, is, in every succeeding game, to imitate more closely the play of the Great Masters; and to endeavor to take his measures with more attention and judgment than in any preceding.

Every player at Chess has defects; many have very great ones. In searching for these one should not treat himself tenderly, and when examining his faults, he should grant himself no quarter.

Particularly should the student cultivate confidence in and rigidly adhere to the standard of skill, as interpreted by that immutable System of Chess-play, of which Morphy is the unapproachable and all-sufficient exponent.

Observing the lack of method displayed by the incompetent Chess-commander, the student of this system will remark with astonishment, the want of plan and the entire absence of co-operation between the various Chessic corps d'armee, which under such leadership are incapable of a general effort.

How dense is such a leader in the selection of a project, how slow and slovenly in its execution; how many opportunities does he suffer to escape him and how many enormous faults does he not commit? To such things, the numerically weaker but more skillful opponent, often is indebted for safety and ultimately for success.

One who is opposed by such blockheads, necessarily must gain advantages continually; for conduct so opposite to all the laws of the Art, is, in itself, sufficient to incur ruin. It is for such negligence on his own part that one often has cause bitterly to reproach himself. But such errors, especially on the part of great players, are exemplary lessons for the student, who from them may learn to be more prudent, circumspect, and wise.

———————

Those who make a mere pastime of Chess, who have no desire for the true benefit of the game, do not deserve information.

Such people are more numerous than may be supposed. They have few coherent ideas and are usually influenced by mere chatter and by writers whose sole excuse is enthusiasm.

These players at the game cannot benefit by example. The follies of others afford them no useful lesson. Each generation of such "wood-shifters," has blindly followed in the footsteps of those preceding and daily is guilty of errors which times innumerable have been fully exposed.

It is the darling habit of such folk to treat the great things in Chess with levity and to dignify those insignificant matters which appertain to the game when used as a plaything.

Such people are merely enthusiastic; usually they are equally frivolous. They do everything from fancy, nothing from design. Their zeal is strong, but they can neither regulate nor control it.

Such bear about their Chessic disabilities in their character. Inflated in good fortune, groveling in adversity, these players never attain to that sage contemplation, which renders the scientific practice of Chess so indescribably beautiful.

There is another class of Chess-players who from mere levity of mind are incapable of steadily pursuing any fixed plan; but who overturn, move by move, even such advantages as their good fortune may have procured. There are others, who, although possessed of great vivacity of mind and eager for information, yet lack that patience necessary to receive instruction.

Lastly, there are not a few whose way of thinking and the validity of whose calculations, depend upon their good or ill digestion.

It is in vain that such people endeavor to divine things beyond their understanding. Hence it is, that among those incapable of thought, or too indolent for mental effort, the game proceeds in easy fashion until routine is over. Afterward, at each move, the most probable conjecture passes for the best reason and victory ultimately rests with him whose blunders are least immediately consequential.

———————

Understanding of high art is dispensed only to the few; the great mass neither can comprehend nor enjoy it. In spite of the good natured Helvetius, all are not wise who wish to be so and men ever will remain what Nature made them. It is impossible for the stream to rise higher than its source.

"The progress of human reason," writes the great Frederic, "is more slow than is imagined; the true cause of which is that most men are satisfied with vague notions of things and but few take time for examination and deep inquiry.

"Some, fettered by prejudice from their infancy, wish not, or are unable to break their chains; others, delighting in frivolity know not a word of mathematics and enjoy life without allowing their pleasures to be interrupted by a moment of reflection. Should one thinking man in a thousand be discovered it will be much; and it is for him that men of talent write.

"The rest naturally are offended, for nothing so enrages the mediocre mind as to be compelled to admit to itself its own inferiority. Consequently, they consign book, author, and reader conjointly to Satan. So much easier is it to condemn than to refute, or to learn."

———————

The early success of many young students does not permit them to observe that they often have departed from the rules of the Art. As they have escaped punishment for their errors, they remain unacquainted with the dangers to which they were exposed. Constant good fortune finally makes them over-confident and they do not suspect it necessary to change their measures, even when in the presence of an able foe.

Thus, the youthful tyro, inconsiderate, inconsistent, and turbulent, and oblivious to the innumerable dangers by which he is surrounded, plays his pieces hither and thither, as fancy and inclination dictate, culling bouquets of the most gorgeous flowers of the imagination; thoughtless of the future and perfectly happy because he cannot reflect.

To reason exactly, the student first must rid his mind of all preconceived notions; he must regard the matter under consideration as a blank sheet of paper, upon which nothing is to be written save those things which by the processes of logic and demonstration, are established as facts.

There is much difference between the Art of Logic and mere conjecture.

The calculations of arithmeticians, though rigorous and exact, are never difficult; because they relate to known quantities and to the palpable objects of nature. But when it is required to argue from combining circumstances, the least ignorance of uncertain and obscure facts breaks the chain and we are deceived every moment.

This is no defect of the understanding, but error arising from plausible ideas, which wear the face of and are too quickly accepted for truth. A long chapter can be written on the different ways in which men lose themselves in their conjectures. Innumerable examples of this are not wanting, and all because they have suffered themselves to be hurried away and thus to be precipitate in drawing their conclusions.

The part that the General, whether in Chess-play or in Warfare, has to act, always is more difficult because he must not permit himself the least mistake, but is bound to behave with prudence and sagacity throughout a long series of intricate processes. A single false deduction, or a movement of the enemy unintelligible to a commander, may lead him to commit an irremediable error; and in cases wherein the situation is beyond comprehension, his ignorance is invincible.

For however extensive the human mind may be, it never is sufficiently so to penetrate those minute combinations necessary to be developed in order to foresee and regulate events, the sequence, utility and even existence of which, depend upon future contingencies.

Incidents which are past, can be explained clearly, because the reasons therefor are manifest. But men easily deceive themselves concerning the future, which, by a veil of innumerable and impenetrable secondary causes, is concealed from the most prying inspection.

In such situations, how puerile are the projects even of the greatest Strategist. To him, as much as to the tyro, is the future hidden; he knows not what shall happen, even on the next move. How then may he foresee those situations which secondary causes later may produce?

Circumstances most often oblige him to act contrary to his wishes; and in the flux and reflux of fortune, it is the part of prudence to conform to system and to act with consistency. It is impossible to foresee all events.

"It is not possible," writes the Count de Saxe, "to establish a system without first being acquainted with the *principles* that must necessarily support it."

In corroboration of this is the opinion of Frederic the Great:

"Condemned by my unfortunate stars to philosophies on contingencies and on probabilities I employ my whole attention to examine the *principle* on which my argument must rest and to procure all possible information on that point. Deprived of such precaution, the edifice I erect, wanting a base, would fall like a house of cards."

Everyone who does not proceed on principle, is inconsistent in his conduct. Equally so, whenever the principle on which one acts is false, *i.e.*, does not apply to the existing situation; all deductions based thereon, if applied to the existing situation, necessarily are false.

"Those principles which the Art of Warfare prescribes, never should be departed from," writes Frederic the Great, "and generals rigidly should adhere to those circumspections and never swerve from implicit obedience to laws, upon whose exact observance depends the safety of their armies and the success of their projects."

Thus the student will clearly see that all other calculations, though never so ingeniously imagined, are of small worth in comparison with comprehension of the use of Strategetic principles. By means of these latter, we are taught to control the raging forces which dominate in the competitive arts and to compel obedience from friend and foe alike.

"To the shame of humanity it must be confessed," writes Frederic the Great, "that what often passes for authority and consequence is mere assumption, used as a cloak to conceal from the layman the extreme of official indolence and stupidity.

"To follow the routine of service, to be busied concerning food and clothing, and to eat when others eat, to fight when others fight, are the whole warlike deeds of the majority and constitute what is called having seen service and grown grey in arms.

"The reason why so many officers remain in a state of mediocrity, is because they neither know, nor trouble themselves to inquire into the causes either of their victories or defeats, although such causes are exceedingly real."

In this connection, writes Polybius, the friend and biographer of Hannibal:

"Having made ourselves masters of the subject of Warfare, we shall no longer ascribe success to Fortune and blindly applaud mere conquerors, as the ignorant do; but we shall approve and condemn from Principle and Reason."

To the Chess-student nothing can be more conclusive than the following:

"My success at Chess-play," writes Paul Morphy, "is due to rigid adherence to fixed rules and Principles."

"Chess is best fought on Principles, free from all deception and trickery."—Wilhelm Steinitz.

GRAND RECONNAISSANCE

"Man can sway the future, only by foreseeing through a clear understanding of the present, to what far off end matters are tending."—Caesar.

"From the erroneous ideas they form in regard to good and evil, the ignorant, the mis-educated and the inexperienced always act without precisely knowing what they ought to desire, or what they ought to fear; and it is not in the end they propose, but in the choice of means, that most deceive themselves."—Aristotle.

GRAND RECONNAISSANCE

"In every situation the principal strategical requirements must clearly be defined and all other things must be subordinated to these considerations."—Frederic the Great.

"One should seek to obtain a knowledge of causes, rather than of effects; and should endeavor to reason from the known, to the unknown."—Euclid.

The province of Grand Reconnaissance is exactly to determine the relative advantages and disadvantages in time, numbers, organization, topography, mobility and position, which appertain to hostile armies contained in the same strategetic plane; and to designate those Corps d'armee by which such advantages are materially expressed.

Those processes which appertain to the making of Grand Reconnaissance, necessarily are argumentative; inasmuch as all the facts never are determinate.

Consequently, talent of the highest order is required for the deducing of conclusions which never can be based upon exact knowledge, and which always must contemplate the presence of numerous unknown quantities.

The responsibilities inherent to Grand Reconnaissance never are to be delegated to, nor thrust upon subordinates. Scouts, spies, and informers of every kind, have their manifold and proper uses, but such uses never rise above furnishing necessary information in regard to topographical, tactical, and logistic details.

The Commander-in-chief alone is presumed to possess knowledge and skill requisite to discern what strategetically is fact and what is not fact; and to ascribe to each fact its proper place and sequence.

Lack of military talent and of Strategetic knowledge, never is more strikingly shown than by negligence or inability in this regard.

Incompetents, ignorant of this truth, and oblivious to its importance, devolve such vital responsibility upon subordinates; and later, these legalized murderers palliate the slaughter of their troops and the national shame by publicly reprimanding men serving at shillings per month, for failing in a service, which were the latter able to perform, would entitle them to the gold epaulets and general's pay, of which their commander is the unfit recipient.

Knowledge of the number, organization, position and movements of the enemy's troops is the basic element for correct calculation in campaign and battle.

Such things to be accurately estimated must be closely inspected. All speculation and all conjecture in regard to these matters is but frivolity.

It is by being precipitate and hasty in making such conclusions, that men are deceived, for to judge rightly of things before they become clearly shown is most difficult.

To act on uncertainty is WRONG.

We do not know all the facts and a single iota of light later on may oblige us to condemn that which we previously have approved.

In the making of Grand Reconnaissance, one always must be wary of placing too much confidence in appearances and in first impressions. Especially must care be taken not to magnify the weaknesses of the hostile army, nor the efficacy of the kindred position.

Also, one never should underrate:

1. The talents of the opposing commander; nor

2. The advantages possessed by the opposing army:

   (a) In numbers,

   (b) In organization,

   (c) In position,

   (d) In topography,

   (e) In time,

   (f) In mobility.

It is a first essential, constantly to note the movements of the enemy, in order to detect his plans and the exact location of his corps.

These things are the only reliable guides for determining the true course of procedure. It must be left to the enemy to show by his movements and the posts which he occupies, the measures he projects for the future, and until these are known, it is not proper to *ACT*. Hence:

PRINCIPLE

All movements of Corps Offensive should be governed by the POSITION of the hostile army, and all movements of Corps Defensive should be governed by the MOVEMENTS of the hostile army.

As soon as the enemy begins a movement, his intentions become clear. It is then possible to make precise calculations.

But be not hasty to build conclusions upon uncertain information and do not take any resolutions until certain what are the numbers, the position, the objectives, and the projects of the enemy.

However interesting an undertaking may appear, one should not be seduced by it while ill-informed of the obstacles to be met and the possibility of not having sufficient force in the theatre of action.

Chimerical schemes should be abandoned at their inception. Reason, instead of extravagancies of the fancy, always must be the guide. Men, most courageous, often undertake fearful difficulties, but impracticable things they leave to lunatics.

In all situations, one must beware of venturing beyond his depth. It is wiser to keep within the limits which the knowledge we possess shall prescribe.

Especially in crises, one must proceed most cautiously until sure information is acquired; for over-haste is exceedingly dangerous, when exact knowledge is lacking of the enemy's numbers, position, and movements.

PRINCIPLE

Situations always should be contemplated as they EXIST, never as they OUGHT to be, or, perhaps, MAY be.

In every important juncture, each step must be profoundly considered; as little as possible should be left to chance.

Particularly, must one never be inflated and rendered careless and negligent by success; nor made spiritless and fearful by reverses. At all times the General should see things only as they are and attempt what is dictated by that Strategetic Principle which dominates the given situation. Fortune often does the rest.

———

"Napoleon bending over and sometimes lying at full length upon his map, with a pair of dividers opened to a distance on the scale of from 17 to 20 miles, equal to 22 to 25 miles over country, and marking the positions of his own and of the hostile armies by sticking into the map pins surmounted by little balls made of diverse colored sealing wax; in the twinkling of an eye calculated those wonderful concentrations of his Corps d'armee upon decisive points and dictated those instructions to his Marshals which in themselves are a title to glory."—Baron de Jomini.

———

MILITARY EXAMPLES

"Phillip, King of Macedonia, is the single confidant of his own secrets, the sole dispenser of his treasure, the most able general of all Greece, the bravest soldier in his army. He foresees and executes everything himself; anticipates events, derives all possible advantages from them and yields to them when to yield is necessary.

His troops are extremely well disciplined, he exercises them incessantly. Always himself at their head, they perform with arms and baggage marches of three hundred stadia with alarming expedition and making no difference between summer or winter, between fatigue and rest.

He takes no step without mature reflection, nor proceeds to a second until he is assured of the success of the first and his operations are always dominated by considerations of time and place."— Apollodorus.

The facility with which one familiar with the Strategetic Art may make Grand Reconnaissance, even of an invisible theatre of action, and may evolve accurate deductions from a mass of inexact and contradictory reports is illustrated by the following practical examples, viz.:

FIRST EXAMPLE.

(From the *New York Journal*, Dec. 26, 1899 By **Franklin K. Young**.)

"The position of the British armies is deplorable.

"With the single exception of Gen. Buller's force, the situation of these bodies of British troops, thus unfortunately circumstanced, is cause for the greatest anxiety.

"Strong indications point to a grand offensive movement on the part of the Boers, with the object of terminating the war in one campaign and by a single blow.

"True, this movement may be but a feint, but if it be a true movement, it is difficult to over-estimate the gravity of the situation of the British in South Africa.

"For if this movement is a true military movement, it shows as clearly as the sun in the sky to those who know the Strategetic Art, that the Boer armies are in transition from the defensive to an offensive plan of campaign, with the purpose of capturing DeArr and from thence advancing in force against the chief British depot, Capetown."

The United States War Department, *Report on the British-Boer War*, published June 14, 1901, contains the following:

(By **Capt. S. L'H. Slocum**, December 25, 1899. U. S. Military Attache with the British Army.)

"I consider the present situation to be the most critical for the English forces, since hostilities began. Should the Boers assume offensive operations, the English armies with their long and thinly guarded lines of communication, would be placed in great jeopardy."

(By **Chas. S. Goldmann**, war correspondent with Gen. Buller and Lord Roberts in the South African Campaign. MacMillan & Co., 1902.)

"Had the defence (of Cape Colony) been entrusted to less capable hands than those of Gen. French, who, with a mere handful of troops succeeded not only in checking the Boer advance, but in driving them back on Colesberg, it is not unreasonable to suppose that the enemy would have been able to push on south and west to Craddock and Hex River range and thus bring about a state of affairs which might have shaken British rule in South Africa to its foundation."

SECOND EXAMPLE.

(*Boston Globe*, Jan. 12, 1900. By **Franklin K. Young**.)

"Lord Roberts' first object will be the rescue of Lord Methuen's army now blockaded near Magersfontein by Gen. Conje.

"As the first step to effect this, the British commander-in-chief at once and with all his force, will occupy the line from Naauwpoort to De Arr. There, he will await the arrival of twenty-two transports now en route from England.

"With these reinforcements, he will advance directly to the Modder River by the route previously taken by Lord Methuen."

(By Chas. S. Goldmann, Sp. Cor. British Army.)

"Slow to recognize their opportunities, the enemy were still in the midst of preparation, when Gen. French reached De Arr. Meanwhile a detachment under Major McCracken occupied Naauwpoort, to which place thirty days' supplies for 3000 men and 1100 animals had been ordered.

"In the ten weeks of fighting which ensued, prior to the arrival of the British main army, Gen. French by his skillful tactics held a powerful force of Boers at bay, checked their descent into the southern part of the colony, defeated their attempt to display the Vierkleur across the cape peninsular, and materially influenced, if not absolutely determined, the entire future of the campaign."

(By Chas. S. Goldmann, Sp. Cor. with British Army.)

"Arriving at Capetown on Jan. 10, Lord Roberts decided that the line of march should lead by way of Bloemfontein to Pretoria, initiating the operation by the concentration of large forces on the Modder River, forming there an advanced base."

THIRD EXAMPLE.

(Boston Globe, Jan. 21, 1900. By Franklin K. Young.)

"It is plain that when the Boers took position at Colenso they prepared their plan for the protection of their flanks; to deny this would be to assume that men who had displayed superb military sagacity were ignorant of the simplest processes of warfare.

"What that plan is will be unfolded very rapidly should Gen. Buller attempt to pierce the line of Boer vedettes posted upon the Spion Kop and concealing as near as can be determined from the present meagre facts, either the Second, or the Fourth Ambuscade.

"In either case it signifies that the Boers are confident of annihilating Gen. Buller's army if it should cross the Tugela.

"About this time the Boers are watching Gen. Warren and his command and watching him intently. Something may happen to him."

(*London Times*, Jan. 22, 1900.)

"On Friday, Jan. 19, Gen. Warren began a long, circuitous march to the westward for the purpose of turning the right of the Boer position.

"This attempt was abandoned on account of the long ridge running from Spion Kop being occupied by the Boers in such strength as to command the entire route.

"Saturday, Jan. 20, Gen. Warren, having crossed the Tugela River with the bulk of his troops, ordered a frontal attack. Our men behaved splendidly under a heavy cross-fire for seven hours. Our casualties were slight. Three lines of rifle fire[1] were visible along the Boer main position."

[1] The Second Ambuscade. Vide "Secret Instructions" of Frederic the Great.

(*British War Office Bulletin*, Jan. 22, 1900.)

"Gen. Warren has been engaged all day chiefly on his left, which he has swung forward a couple of miles."

(Signed)   *Buller.*

(*British War Office Bulletin*, Jan. 24, 1900.)

"Gen. Warren holds the position he gained two days ago. The Boer position is on higher ground than ours and can be approached only over bare and open slopes. An attempt will be made tonight to seize Spion Kop."

(Signed)   *Buller.*

(*British War Office Bulletin*, Jan. 25, 1900.)

"Gen. Warren's troops last night occupied Spion Kop, surprising the small[2] garrison which fled."

(Signed)   *Buller.*

[2] Merely the outposts and vedettes of the Second Ambuscade.

(*British War Office Bulletin*, Jan. 26, 1900.)

"Gen. Warren's garrison, I am sorry to say, I find this morning had in the night abandoned Spion Kop."

(Signed)   *Buller.*

(*British War Office Bulletin*, Jan. 28, 1900.)

"I decided that a second attack on Spion Kop was useless[3] and that the enemy's right was too strong to allow me to force it. Accordingly I decided to withdraw the troops to the south side of the Tugela River."

(Signed)   Buller.

[3] The proffer of an untenable post always is the bait of the Second Ambuscade.

(London Daily Mail, Jan. 29, 1900.)

"The richest and what was hitherto considered the most powerful nation in the world is today in the humiliating position of seeing its armies beaten back with heavy losses by two small states."

FOURTH EXAMPLE.

(Boston Globe, Feb. 16, 1900, by Franklin K. Young.)

"Lord Roberts' communications for nearly two hundred miles are exposed to the attack of an enemy, who at any moment is liable to capture and destroy his supply and ammunition trains and to reduce the British army to a condition wherein it will be obliged to fight a battle under most disadvantageous circumstances."

(From United States War Department Report on the British Boer War. By Capt. S. L'H. Slocum, U. S. Attache with British Army.)

"Feb. 15, 1900. The main supply park of the army was attacked by the enemy near Watervale Drift.

"This park consisted of one hundred ox-wagons containing rations and one hundred more wagons filled with ammunition. One hundred and fifty of these wagons and three thousand oxen were captured by the Boers.

"The loss of these rations and munitions was a most serious blow. Lord Roberts was here confronted by a crisis which would have staggered and been the undoing of many commanders-in-chief placed as he was.

"He was in the enemy's country, cut off from his base of supplies on the railroad and with an unknown number of the enemy in his rear and upon his line of communication. His transport was nearly all captured and his army was suddenly reduced to three days full rations on the eve of a great movement and the country afforded no food whatever. The crisis still further developed when a courier brought the report that the Boers were in position at Watervale Drift and commanding the ford with artillery."

FIFTH EXAMPLE.

(*Boston Globe*, Feb. 25, 1900. By **Franklin K. Young**.)

"There is reason to believe that should worse come to worse, the Boer Army, should it be compelled to abandon its position, will be able to save its personnel by a rapid flight across the Modder. Of course, in this case, the Boers would lose their supplies and cannon."

(From United States War Department, *Report on the British Boer War*. By **Capt. S. L'H. Slocum**, U. S. Attache, with British Army.)

"The enemy, under Cronje, with all his transport was in all practical effect surrounded, although by abandoning his wagons and supplies, a large number of the Boers undoubtedly could have escaped."

(*Boston Sunday Times*, March, 1900. By **Franklin K. Young**.)

"Cronje's conduct was heroic and imbecile in the extreme. As the commander on the ground he is entitled to all the glory and must assume all the blame. One of the ablest of the Boer generals, he is the only one in the whole war to make a mistake.

"Cronje's first duty was to decide whether he should stand or run; he decided to run, which was proper, but having so decided he should have run at once and not have stopped running until safe on the north bank of the Vaal River.

"Properly he sent his siege guns and trains off to the north across the Vaal and improperly held his position in force on the British front, instead of withdrawing his personnel after his material.

"This blunder, like all blunders of a commander-in-chief, quickly produced blunders by his subordinates. Commander Ferrera permitted French to get around Cronje's left flank without a battle. The presence of this force on his rear cut Cronje off from his natural line of retreat across the Vaal and compelled him to flee toward Bloemfontein.

"Even now Cronje was all right; he easily and brilliantly out-manoeuvred the British and gained the protection of the Modder River. But a second time he blundered. Instead of first executing Ferrera and then abandoning everything and devoting all his efforts to saving his men, he neglected an obvious and imperative military duty and clung to his slow-moving cannon and wagons.

"Finally he took position on the Modder and resolved to fight the whole British army. This was fatal.

"Then for the fourth time he blundered. Having made his decision to fight he should not have surrendered to the British on the anniversary of Majuba

Hill. On the contrary, surrounded by the mightiest army the British empire ever put in the field and enveloped in the smoke of a hundred cannon, Cronje, upon a rampart formed by his dead army and with his last cartridge withstanding the destroyers of his country, would have presented to posterity a more spectacular and seemingly a more fitting termination of the career of the Lion of South Africa."

"Mere hope of attaining their desires, coupled with ignorance of the processes necessary to their accomplishment, is the common delusion and the certain destruction of the inexperienced."—Plato.

ORGANIZATION

"To employ in warfare an uninstructed people is to destroy the nation."—Chinese Saying.

Antiochus, King of Syria, reviewing his immense but untrained and undisciplined army at Ephesus, asked of Hannibal, "if they were not enough for the Romans."

"Yes," replied the great Carthagenian, "enough to glut the bloodthirstiness, even of the Romans."

"A man in the vigor of life and capable of sustaining the heaviest fatigues, but untrained in warfare, is fitted not to bear arms, but to bear baggage."—Timoleon.

ORGANIZATION

"The chief distinction between an army and a mob is the good order and discipline of the former and the disorderly behavior of the latter."—Washington.

"It is the duty of the commander-in-chief frequently to assemble the most prudent and experienced of his generals and to consult with them as to the state of his own and of the enemies'troops.

"He must examine which army has the better weapons, which is the better trained and disciplined; superior in condition and most resolute in emergencies.

"He must note whether himself or the adversary has the superior infantry, cavalry or artillery, and particularly must he discern any marked lack in quantity and quality of men or horses, and any difference in equipment of those corps which necessarily will be or because of such reason, advantageously may be opposed to each other.

"Advantages in Organization determine the field of battle to be preferred, which latter should be selected with the view of profiting to the uttermost by the use of specially equipped corps, to whom the enemy is not able to oppose similar troops.

"If a general finds himself superior to his enemy he must use all means to bring on an engagement, but if he sees himself inferior, he must avoid battle and endeavor to succeed by surprises, stratagems and ambuscades; which last skillfully managed often have gained the victory over foemen superior in numbers and in strength."—*Vergetius.*

―――――――――――

Advantage in Organization consists in having one or more Corps d'armee which in equipment or in composition are so superior to the hostile corps to which they may become opposed, as entails to them exceptional facilities for the execution of those major tactical evolutions that appertain to any tactical area made up of corresponding geometric or sub-geometric symbols.

PRINCIPLE

Advantage in Organization determines the choice of a prospective battlefield; and the latter always should be composed of those tactical areas which permit of the fullest exercise of the powers peculiar to kindred corps d'armee.

Every corps d'armee thus especially equipped should be constantly and energetically employed in the prospective battle; and usually it will eventuate as the Prime Tactical Factor in the decisive Major Tactical evolution.

———

Notions most mistaken prevail in regard to the Pawns and Pieces of the Chessboard.

To suppose that the Chessmen *per se* may be utilized to typify the different arms of the military service is a fallacy.

Many unfamiliar with the technicalities of Strategetic Science delude themselves that the Pawns, on account of their slow and limited movements properly are to be regarded as Infantry; that the Knights because topped by horses' heads thereby qualify as light Cavalry; the Bishops, for reasons unknown, often are held to represent Artillery; the Rooks, because of their swift, direct and far-reaching movements are thought to duplicate heavy Cavalry; while the Queen, in most of these unsophisticated philosophies, is supposed to constitute a Reserve.

Nothing can be further from the truth than such assumptions.

As a fundamental of military organization applied to Chessplay, each Chesspiece typifies in itself a complete Corps d'armee. Each of these Chessic corps d'armee is equal to every other in strength, but all differ, more or less, in construction and in facilities, essential to the performance of diverse and particular duties.

Thus it is that while every Chesspiece represents a perfectly appointed and equally powerful body of troops, these corps d'armee in Chessplay as in scientific warfare are not duplicates, except to others of their own class. Each of these corps d'armee is made up of Infantry, Cavalry and Artillery in correct proportion to the service they are to perform and such proportions are determined not by simple arithmetic, but by those deployments, developments, evolutions, and manoeuvres, which such corps d'armee is constructed promptly and efficiently to execute.

The Chessmen, therefore, do not as individuals represent either infantry, cavalry or artillery.

But in the same manner as the movements of troops over the surface of the earth, exemplify the attributes of the three kindred grand columns in the greater logistics of a campaign; so do those peculiarities which appertain to the moves of the different Chesspieces exemplify the action of the three chief arms of the military service; either singly or in combination against given points in given times, in the evolutions of the battlefield, viz.:

CORPS D'ARMEE EN MARCH.

The march of:

(a) Infantry, alone, or of

(b) Cavalry, alone, or of

(c) Artillery, alone, or of

(d) Infantry and Cavalry, or of

(e) Infantry and Artillery, or of

(f) Cavalry and Artillery, or of

(g) Infantry, Cavalry and Artillery,

is indicated by the movement of any Chesspiece from a given point to an unoccupied adjacent point.

The march of:

(a) Cavalry, alone, or of

(b) Artillery, alone, or of

(c) Cavalry and Artillery,

is indicated by the movement of any Chesspiece from a given point to an unoccupied point, *not* an adjacent point.

CORPS D'ARMEE EN ASSAULT.

The *Charge of Infantry* is indicated by the movement of any Chesspiece from a given point to an occupied adjacent point; posting itself thereon and capturing the adverse piece there located.

The *Charge of Cavalry* is indicated by the movement of any Chesspiece from a given point to an occupied point *not* an adjacent point; posting itself thereon and capturing the adverse piece there located.

CORPS D'ARMEE FIRE EFFECT.

Infantry:

Offensive Fire Effect. Compelling an adverse piece to withdraw from its post upon an adjacent occupied point.

Defensive Fire Effect. Preventing an adverse piece from occupying an adjacent unoccupied point.

Artillery:

Offensive Fire Effect. Compelling an adverse piece to withdraw from its post upon an occupied point not an adjacent point.

Defensive Fire Effect. Preventing an adverse piece from occupying an unoccupied point not an adjacent point.

CHESSIC CORPS D'ARMEE.

The *Corps d'armee of the Chessboard* are divided into two classes: viz.:

I. Corps of Position.

II. Corps of Evolution.

CORPS D'ARMEE OF POSITION.

"The Pawns are the soul of Chess; upon their good or bad arrangement depends the gain or loss of the game."—Philidor.

The eight Pawns, by reason of their limited movements, their inability to move backward and the peculiarity of their offensive and defensive powers, are best adapted of the Chesspieces to perform those functions which in the Military Art appertain to Corps of Position.

Each Corps of Position has its particular and designated Point of Mobilization and of Development, which differ with the various Strategic Fronts.

Upon each Corps of Position devolves the duties of maintaining itself as a consistent integer of the established, or projected kindred Pawn Integral; as a possible kindred Promotable Factor and as a Point of Impenetrability upon the altitude of an opposing Pawn.

Corps of Position take their individual appelation from their posts in a given formation, viz.:

1. Base Corps.

2. Pivotal Corps.

3. Minor Vertex Corps.

4. Minor Corps Aligned.

5. Major Vertex Corps.

6. Major Corps Aligned.

7. Corps Enpotence.

8. Minor Corps Enceinte.

9. Major Corps Enceinte.

10. Corps Echeloned.

11. Corps En Appui.

12. Base Corps Refused.

13. Pivotal Corps Refused.

14. Minor Vertex Corps Refused.

15. Minor Corps Aligned Refused.

16. Major Vertex Corps Refused.

17. Major Corps Aligned Refused.

18. Major Corps Refused Enpotence.

19. Corps en Major Crochet.

20. Corps en Minor Crochet.

21. Corps en Crochet Aligned.

22. Corps Doubly Aligned.

23. Grand Vertex Corps.

The above formations by Corps of Position are described and illustrated in detail in preceding text-books by the author, entitled:

The Minor Tactics of Chess.

The Grand Tactics of Chess.

The normal use of Corps of Position is limited to Lines of Mobilization, of Development and to the Simple Line of Manoeuvre.

CORPS D'ARMEE OF EVOLUTION.

"Every man in Alexander's army is so well trained and obedient that at a single word of command, officers and soldiers make any movement and execute any evolution in the art of warfare.

"Only such troops as themselves can check their career and oppose their bravery and expertness."—Caridemus.

The eight Pieces, by reason of their ability to move in all directions, the scope of their movements and the peculiar exercises of their offensive and defensive powers, are best adapted of the Chesspieces to perform those functions which in the Military Art appertain to Corps of Evolution.

Corps of Evolution acting offensively, take their individual appelations from the points which constitute their objective in the true Strategetic Horizon, viz.:

1. Corps of the Right.

2. Corps of the Centre.

3. Corps of the Left.

Corps of Evolution acting defensively, take their individual appelations from the particular duties they are required to perform, viz.:

1. Supporting Corps.

2. Covering Corps.

3. Sustaining Corps.

4. Corps of Impenetrability.

5. Corps of Resistance.

The normal use of Corps of Evolution is limited to Lines of Manoeuvre. When acting on a Simple Line of Manoeuvre, a Corps of Evolution may deploy on the corresponding Line of Mobilization; but it has nothing in common with the Line of Development, which latter appertains exclusively to Corps of Position.

Any corps d'armee, whether of Position or of Evolution may be utilized upon a Line of Operations.

THE KING.

Regarded as a Chessic Corps d'armee, the King marches as infantry, cavalry and artillery; but it attacks as infantry exclusively and never as cavalry or artillery.

Although every situation upon the Chessboard contemplates the presence of both Kings, either, or neither, or both, may, or may not be present in any given Strategetic Horizon.

Whenever the King is present in a given Strategetic Horizon the effect of his co-operation is mathematically outlined, thus:

I. At his maximum of efficiency, the King occupies the centre of a circle of one point radius. His offensive power is equally valid against all eight points contained in his circumference, but his defensive power is valid for the support from a minimum of one point to a maximum of five points.

II. At his medium of efficiency the King occupies the centre of a semi-circle of one point radius. His offensive power is valid against all five points contained in his semi-circumference, and his defensive power is valid for the support from a minimum of one, to a maximum of five points.

III. At his minimum of efficiency, the King occupies the centre of a quadrant of one point radius. Both his offensive and his defensive powers are valid against all three points contained in his segment.

THE QUEEN.

Regarded as a Chessic Corps d'armee the Queen marches and attacks as infantry, cavalry and artillery.

Either, neither, or both Queens may be present in any given Strategetic Horizon; and whenever present the effect of her co-operation mathematically is outlined, viz.:

At her maximum of efficiency the Queen occupies the common vertex of one or more unequal triangles, whose aggregate area is from a minimum of 21 to a maximum of 27 points. Her offensive power is equally valid against all of these points; but her defensive power is valid for the support from a minimum of one point to a maximum of five points.

THE ROOK.

Regarded as a Chessic Corps d'armee the Rook marches and attacks as infantry, cavalry and artillery.

From one to four Rooks may be present in any given Strategetic Horizon; and whenever present the effect of its co-operation mathematically is outlined, viz.:

At her maximum of efficiency, the Rook occupies the common angle of four quadrilaterals, whose aggregate area always is 14 points. The Offensive Power of the Rook is equally valid against all these points, but his defensive power is valid for the support of only two points.

THE BISHOP.

Regarded as a Chessic Corps d'armee, the Bishop marches and attacks as infantry, cavalry and artillery.

From one to four Bishops may be present in any Strategetic Horizon; and whenever present the effect of its co-operation mathematically is outlined, viz.:

At its maximum of efficiency, the Bishop occupies the common vertex of four unequal triangles, having a maximum of 13 and a minimum of 9 points. His offensive power is valid against all of these points but his defensive power is valid only for the support of two points.

KNIGHT.

Regarded as a Chessic Corps d'armee the Knight marches and attacks as cavalry and artillery.

From one to four Knights may be present in any given Strategetic Horizon; and whenever present the effect of its co-operation mathematically is outlined, viz.:

At its maximum of efficiency, the Knight occupies the centre of an octagon of two points radius, having a minimum of two points and a maximum of eight points area. His offensive power is equally valid against all of these eight points, but his defensive power is valid for the support of only one point.

THE PAWN.

Regarded as a Chessic Corps d'armee, the Pawn at its normal post marches as infantry and cavalry. Should an adverse corps, however, take post within the kindred side of the Chessboard; that Pawn upon whose altitude the adverse Piece appears, at once loses its equestrian attributes and marches and attacks exclusively as infantry.

Located at any other point than at its normal post, the Pawn is composed exclusively of infantry and never acts either as cavalry or artillery.

From one to eight Pawns may be present in any Strategetic Horizon; and whenever present the effect of its co-operation mathematically is outlined as follows:

At its maximum of efficiency the Pawn occupies the vertex of a triangle of two points. Its offensive power is equally valid against both of these points; but its defensive power is valid for the support of only one point.

POTENTIAL COMPLEMENTS.

Subjoined is a table of the potential complements of the Chesspieces.

The King	6⁹⁄₁₆	units.
The Queen	22¼	″
The Rook	14	″
The Bishop	8¾	″
The Knight	5¼	″
The Pawn	1½	″

The student clearly should understand that this table does not indicate prowess, but relates exclusively to normal facilities for bringing force into action.

———

The relative advantage in Organization possessed by one army over an opposing army always can be determined by the following, viz.:

RULE.

1. Above a line, set down in order those abbreviations which properly designate the White corps d'armee present in a given Strategetic Situation; and below the line, set down those abbreviations which in like manner designate the Black corps d'armee, viz.:

$$\frac{K+Q+R+R+P+P+P+P}{K+Q+R+B+P+P+P+P+P}$$

2. Cancel all like symbols and resolve the unlike symbols remaining, into their respective Potential complements, viz.:

$$\frac{R}{B+P} = \frac{}{8\frac{3}{4} + 1\frac{1}{2}} = \frac{14}{10\frac{1}{4}}$$

3. Subtract the lesser Potential total from the greater and the difference will be the relative advantage in Organization.

4. To utilize the relative advantage in Organization select a battlefield in which the Strategic Key, the Tactical Keys and the Points of Command of the True Strategetic Horizon are situated upon the perimeters of those geometric and sub-geometric symbols which appertain to the corps d'armee whose superior potentiality is established by Section 2.

5. To neutralize the relative disadvantage in Organization, occupy the necessary posts upon the battlefield selected in such a manner that the kindred decisive points are situated *not* upon the perimeters of the geometric and sub-geometric symbols appertaining to the adverse corps d'armee of superior potentiality; while the adverse decisive points *are* situated upon the perimeters of the geometric and sub-geometric symbols which appertain to the kindred corps d'armee of inferior potentiality.

MILITARY EXAMPLES

"Men habituated to luxury cannot contend with an army accustomed to fatigue and inured to want."—Caesar.

"That wing with which you propose to engage the enemy should be composed of your best troops."—Epaminondas.

The *Sacred Band* of the Thebans was composed of men selected for valor and character. Epaminondas called them *Comrades* and by honorable rewards and distinctions induced them to bear without murmur the hardest fatigues and to confront with intrepidity the greatest dangers.

At Leuctra (371 B.C.) and again at Mantinea (362 B.C.) the right wing of the Lacedaemonian Army, composed exclusively of Spartans and for six hundred years invincible, was overthrown and destroyed by the Sacred Band led by Epaminondas.

This formidable body of Theban warriors was massacred by Alexander the Great at the Battle of Chaeronea (338 B.C.)

The *Macedonian Phalanx* was devised by Philip, King of Macedon. It was made up of heavy infantry accoutred with cuirass, helmet, greaves, and shield. The principal weapon was a pike twenty-four feet long.

The Phalanx had a front of two hundred and fifty-six files and a depth of sixteen ranks. A file of sixteen men was termed Lochos; two files were called Dilochie; four files made a Tetrarchie; eight files a Taxiarchie and thirty-two of the last constituted a simple Phalanx of 4096 men. A grand Phalanx had a front of one thousand and twenty-four files and a depth of sixteen ranks. It was made up of four simple Phalanxes and contained 16,384 men.

With this formation of his infantry, Alexander the Great, when eighteen years of age, destroyed the Allied Athenian—Theban—Boeotian army at Chaeronea, the hosts of Persia at the river Grancius (334 B.C.) at Issus (333 B.C.) and Arbela (331 B.C.) and conquered Porus, King of India at the Hydaspes (326 B.C.).

The *Spanish Heavy Cavalry* and *Nubian Infantry* of Hannibal was a reproduction of that Macedonian organization whereby Alexander the Great had conquered the world.

With this formation Hannibal maintained himself for fifteen years in the richest provinces of Italy and destroyed seven Roman armies, at the Trebia (218 B.C.) at Lake Trasymenus (217 B.C.) at Cannae (216 B.C.) and at Herdonea (212 B.C.) at Herdonea (210 B.C.) at Locri (208 B.C.) and at Apulia (208 B.C.).

At Zama (202 B.C.) Hannibal's effacement as a military factor was directly due to his lack of that organization which had been the instrument of his previous successes; a circumstance thus commented on by the victorious Roman commander, Scipio Africanus;

"Hitherto I have been opposed by an army without a general; now they send against me a General without an army."

———

The *Tenth Legion* of Caesar was the quintessence of that perfection in elementary tactics devised by the Romans to accord with the use of artillery.

The fundamentals of minor tactics as elucidated by Epaminondas and exploited by Alexander the Great and Hannibal are unchanged in the Legion, but by subdivision of the simple Phalanx into ten Cohorts, a necessary and maximum gain in mobility was effected.

The Roman Legion consisted of 6100 infantry and 726 cavalry, divided into the Militarain Cohort of 1105 heavy foot, 132 Cuirassiers and nine ordinary Cohorts, each containing 555 heavy foot and 66 Cuirassiers. The Legion was drawn up in three lines; the first of which was termed Principes, the second Hastati, and the third Triarii. The infantry were protected by helmet, cuirass, greaves and shield; their arms were a long sword, a short sword, five javelins and two large spears.

With this formation Caesar over-run Spain, Gaul, Germany, Britain, Africa, Greece, and Italy. The Scots alone withstood him and the ruins of a triple line of Roman entrenchments extending from the North to the Irish Seas to this day mark the southern boundary of the Scottish Highlands and the northern limit of Roman dominion.

At Pharseleus, Pompey made the inexplicable blunder of placing his best troops in his right wing, which was covered by the river Enipeus and inferior troops on his left wing which was in the air. By its first charge, the Tenth Legion destroyed the latter, outflanked the entire Pompeian army, drove it backward into the river and single handed won for Caesar undisputed dominion of the Earth.

———

The *Scots Volunteers* of Gustavus Adolphus consisted of two brigades aggregating about 12,000 foot, made up of Scottish gentlemen who for various reasons were attracted to the Continental Wars.

At Leipsic, (Sept. 7, 1631) 20,000 Saxons, constituting one-half of the allied Protestant army, were routed at the first charge, put to flight and never seen again. Tilly's victorious right wing then turned upon the flank of the King's army. Three regiments of the Scots Volunteers on foot held in check in open field 12,000 of the best infantry and cavalry in Europe, until Gustavus had destroyed the Austrian main body and hastened to their aid with the Swedish heavy cavalry.

The Castle of Oppenheim was garrisoned by 800 Spanish infantry. Gustavus drew up 2,000 Swedes to escalade the place. Thirty Scots Volunteers, looking on observed that the Spaniards, intently watching the King had neglected to guard the opposite side of the fortress. Beckoning to their aid about a hundred of their comrades, they scaled the wall, captured the garrison and opened the gates to the king. Gustavus entered on foot, hat in hand. "My brave Scots," said he, "you carry in your scabbards, the key to every castle in Europe."

―――――――

The *Van-Guard* of Frederic the Great is the perfect adaptation of the minor tactics of Epaminondas to gunpowder. This choice body was made up of the best troops in the army divided into infantry, cuirassiers, dragoons and light artillery.

The Van-Guard, a miniature army in itself, always marched between the main body and the enemy; it always led in the attack, followed by that wing containing the best soldiers, in two lines; and supported by the heavy cavalry on that flank.

At Rosbach (Nov. 5, 1757) the Prussian Van-Guard, composed of 4,800 infantry, 2,500 cavalry and 30 guns, annihilated 70,000 French regular troops, by evolutions so rapidly executed that the Prussian main army was unable to overtake either pursuers or pursued and had no part in the battle, other than as highly interested spectators.

The *Continentals* of the Revolutionary army under Washington were made up of troops enlisted for the war and trained by Baron von Steuben, a Major-General in the Prussian service, who had served throughout the Seven Years War under Frederic the Great.

The Continentals, without firing a shot, carried by assault, Stony Point (July 16, 1779), Paulus Hook (July 20, 1779) and the British intrenchments at Yorktown (Oct. 19, 1781). Of these troops, the Baron von Steuben writes:

"I am satisfied with having shown to those who understand the Art of Warfare, an American army worthy of their approbation; officers who know their profession and who would do honor to any army in Europe; an infantry such as England has never brought into the field, soldiers temperate, well-drilled and obedient and the equal of any in the world."

The *Consular Guard* was the reproduction of the Van Guard of Frederic the Great, but its sphere of action was strangely restricted by Bonaparte, who, instead of placing his best troops in the front of his army, as is the practice of all other of the Great Captains; subordinated their functions to that of a reserve and to personal attendance upon himself.

This Corps d'elite was but once notably in action; at Marengo (June 14, 1800) it undoubtedly saved the day for France, by maintaining the battle until the arrival of Gen. Desaix and his division.

The *Imperial Guard* of Napoleon was the development of the Consular Guard of Bonaparte. Under the Empire the Guard became an independent army, consisting of light and heavy infantry, horse and field artillery, cuirassiers, dragoons, hussars and chasseurs, and composed of the best troops in the French service.

The functions of this fine body, like that of its prototype, was limited to the duties of a reserve and to attendance upon the person of the Emperor; and perhaps next to announcement of victory, Napoleon's favorite bulletin always read, "The Imperial Guard was not engaged."

Many were the unavailing remonstrances made by his advisors against this policy, which judged by the practice of the great masters of warfare, is putting the cart before the horse; and seemingly is that speck of cloud in Napoleon's political sky, which properly may be deemed a precursor of St.Helena.

At Austerlitz (Dec. 2, 1805), the cuirassiers of the French Imperial Guard routed a like body of Russian cavalry. At Eylau (Nov. 7, 1807) the Guard, as at Marengo again saved the day, after the corps d'armee of Soult and Angereau had been destroyed, by maintaining the battle until the arrival of Ney and Davoust. In the retreat from Russia (1812) the Guard then numbering 64,000 men was nearly destroyed. What was left of it won at Ligny (June 16, 1815), Napoleon's last victory and at Waterloo (June 18, 1815), one of its two surviving divisions covered the flight of the French army, while the other escorted Napoleon in safety to Paris.

———

The *Royal Prussian Guard*, under Von Moltke, was organized and utilized in accord with the teachings of Frederic the Great.

Its most notable achievement occurred in the campaign of 1870. The right flank of the French having been turned by the battle of Woerth (Aug. 4, 1870) and Marshal MacMahon's army being driven to the westward, it became the paramount object of Von Moltke to seize the country in rear of Metz and thus prevent the retreat of Marshall Bazine across the Moselle River.

The Royal Prussian Guard out-marching both friends and enemies first reached the Nancy road (Aug. 18, 1870) and until the German corps reached the battlefield this body of picked troops successfully withstood the assault of nearly the entire French army. In the first half-hour the Guard lost 8,000 men.

As the result of all this, Marshal Bazine with 150,000 men was forced back into and taken in the intrenched camp at Metz; and the Emperor Napoleon III, Marshal MacMahon and a second French army of 140,000 men was captured at Sedan (Sept. 1, 1870), in an attempt to rescue Marshal Bazine.

———

"I must tell you beforehand this will be a bloody touch. Tilly has a great army of old lads with iron faces that dare look an enemy in the eye; they are confident of victory, have never been beaten and do not know what it means to fly. Tilly tells his men he will beat me and the old man is as likely to do it as to say it."—Gustavus Adolphus.

"Tilly's men were rugged, surly fellows; their faces mangled by wounds and scars had an air of hardy courage. I observed of them that their clothes were always dirty, their armor rusty from winter storms and bruised by musket-balls, their weapons sharp and bright. They were used to camp in the open fields and to sleep in the frosts and rain. The horses like the men were strong and hardy and knew by rote their exercises. Both men and animals so well understood the trade of arms that a general command was sufficient; every man was fit to command the whole, and all evolutions were performed in order and with readiness, at a note of the trumpet or a motion of their banners.

"The 7th of Sept. (1631) before sunrise, the Swedish army marched from Dieben to a large field about a mile from Leipsic, where we found old Tilly's army in full battalia in admirable order, which made a show both glorious and terrible.

"Tilly, like a fair gamester, had taken up but one side of the plain, and left the other side clear and all the avenues open to the King's approach, nor did he stir to the charge until the Swedish army was fully drawn up and was advancing toward him. He had with him 44,000 old soldiers and a better army I believe never was so soundly beaten....

"Then was made a most dreadful slaughter, and yet there was no flying. Tilly's men might be killed or knocked down, but no man turned his back, nor would give an inch of ground, save as they were marched, wheeled, or retreated by their officers.... About six o'clock the field was cleared of the enemy except at one place on the King's front, where some of them rallied; and though they knew that all was lost, they would take no quarter, but fought it out to the last man, being found dead the next day in rank and file as they were drawn up."

Perfection in Organization is attained when troops instantly and intelligently act according to order and execute with exactness and precision any and every prescribed evolution.

TOPOGRAPHY

"Let us not consider where we shall give battle, but where we may gain the victory."—Phocion.

"There can be no discretion in a movement which forsakes the advantage in ground."—Gustavus Adolphus.

"That battlefield is best which is adapted to the full use of the chief constituents of your army and unfavorable to the mass of the enemy."—Napoleon.

TOPOGRAPHY

"The ground is the CHESSBOARD of we cannibals; and it is the selection and use made of it, that decides the knowledge or the ignorance of those by whom it is occupied."—Frederic the Great.

The highest use of Topography consists in reducing a superior adverse force to the inferior force, by minimizing the radius of action of the hostile Corps d'armee.

This is effected by so posting the kindred corps that in the resulting Strategetic Horizons, impassable natural barriers are presented to the march of hostile corps toward their respective objectives.

On the surface of the earth such natural barriers are formed by mountains, rivers, lakes, swamps, forests, deserts, the ocean, and the boundaries of neutral States.

On the Chess-board these topographical conditions are typified by peculiarities and limitations in the movements of the Chess-pieces, viz.:

I. The sides of the Chess-board which terminate all movements of the chess pieces.

II. That limitation of the movements of the Chesspieces which makes it impossible for them to move other than in straight lines.

III. The inability of the Queen to move on obliques.

IV. The inability of the Rook to move either on obliques or on diagonals.

V. The inability of the Bishop to move either on obliques, verticals, or horizontals.

VI. The inability of the Knight to move either on diagonals, verticals, or horizontals, and the limitation of its move to two squares distance.

VII. The inability of the Pawn to move either on obliques or horizontals, and the limitation of its first move to two squares and of its subsequent moves to one square.

VIII. The limitation of the King's move to one square.

These limitations and impediments to the movements of the Chess-pieces, are equivalent in Chess-play to obstacles interposed by Nature to the march of troops over the surface of the earth.

Prefect Generalship, in its calculations, so combines these insurmountable barriers with the relative positions of the contending armies, that the kindred army becomes at every vital point the superior force.

This effect is produced by merely causing rivers and mountains to take the place of kindred Corps d'armee.

It is only by the study of Chessic topography that the tremendous problems solved by the chess player become manifest:

Instead of calculations limited to one visible and unchangeable Chess-board of sixty-four squares, the divinations of the Chess-master comprehend and harmonize as many invisible Chess-boards as there are Chess-pieces contained in the Topographical Zone.

Furthermore, all these surfaces differ to the extent and in conformity to that particular sensible horizon, appertaining to the Chess-piece from which it emanates.

The enormous difficulties of Chess-play, like those of warfare, arise from the necessity of combining in a single composite topographical horizon, all those differing, sensible horizons which appertain, not merely to the kindred, but also to the hostile corps; and to do this in such a manner, as to minimize the hostile powers for offence and defence, by debarring one or more of the hostile pieces from the true Strategetic Horizon.

To divide up the enemy's force, by making natural barriers take the place of troops, is the basis of those processes which dominate Grand Manoeuvres.

Of all the deductions of Chess-play and of warfare, such combinations of Strategy and Topography are the most subtle and intangible. The highest talent is required in its interpretation, and mastery of it, more than of any other branch of Strategetics, proclaims the great Captain at war, or at chess.

TOPOGRAPHY OF THE KING

From the view-point of the *King*, the surface of the Chess-board takes on the topographical aspect of a vast expanse of open, level country.

This vista is void of insurmountable natural obstacles, other than the sides and extremities. The latter collectively may be regarded, for strategical purposes, either as the Ocean, or the boundaries of neutral States.

To the King, this vast territory is accessible in all directions. At his pleasure he may move to and occupy either of the sixty-four squares of the Chess-board, in a minimum of one and in a maximum of seven moves. The only obstacles to his march are distance and the opposition of an enemy.

The Strategical weakness of the Topographical Horizon peculiar to the King arises from its always taking on and maintaining the physical form of a plain. Consequently it is vulnerable to attack from all sides and what is far worse, it readily is commanded and from a superior topographical post, by every adverse piece, except the King and Pawn.

Thus, the hostile Queen, without being attacked in return, may enfilade the King along all verticals, horizontals and diagonals; the Rooks, along all verticals and horizontals; the Bishops, along all diagonals of like color; and the Knights along all obliques.

TOPOGRAPHY OF THE QUEEN

From the view-point of the *Queen*, the surface of the Chess-board takes on the topographical aspect of a series of wide, straight valleys separated by high, impassable mountain ranges, unfordable rivers, and impenetrable forests and morasses. These valleys, which number never less than three, nor more than eight, in the same group, are of varying length and always converge upon and unite with each other at the point occupied by the Queen.

These valleys contained in the Queen's topographical horizon may be classified, viz.:

Class I, consists of those groups made up of three valleys.

Class II, of those groups made up of five valleys.

Class III, of those groups made up of eight valleys of lesser area; and

Class IV, of those groups made up of eight valleys of greater area.

Groups of the first class always have an area of twenty points; those of the second have an area of twenty-three points; those of the third have an area of twenty-five points, and those of the fourth have an area of twenty-seven points. Such areas always are exclusive of that point upon which the Queen is posted.

Although impassable natural barriers restrict the movement of the Queen to less than one-half of the Topographical Zone, these obstacles always are intersected by long stretches of open country formed by intervening valleys.

Hence, the march of this most mobile of the Chesspieces always is open either in three, five, or eight directions, and it always is possible for her, unless impeded by the interference of kindred or hostile corps, to reach any desired point on the Chess-board in two moves.

The weakness peculiar to the Topographical Horizon which appertains to the Queen, originates in the fact that it never commands the origins of obliques. Consequently, every post of the Queen, is open to unopposed attack by the hostile Knights.

TOPOGRAPHY OF THE ROOK

From the view-point of the *Rook*, the surface of the Chess-board takes on a topographical aspect which varies with the post occupied.

Placed at either R1 or R8 the Rook occupies the central point of a great valley, 15 points in length, which winds around the slope of an immense and inaccessible mountain range. This latter, in extent, includes the remainder of the Topographical Zone.

With the Rook placed at R2 or R7, this great mountain wall becomes pierced by a long valley running at right angles to the first, but the area open to the movement of the Rook is not increased.

Placed at Kt2, B3, K4, or Q4, the Rook becomes enclosed amid impassable natural barriers. But although in such cases it always occupies the point of union of four easily traversed although unequal valleys, its area of movement is neither increased nor diminished, remaining always at fourteen points open to occupation.

Unless impeded by the presence of kindred or adverse corps on its logistic radii, the Rook always may move either in two, three, or four directions, and it may reach any desired point on the Chess-board in two moves.

The weakness peculiar to the Topographical Horizon of the Rook lies in the fact that it never commands the origins of diagonals or obliques. Hence it is open to unopposed attack along the first from adverse Queen, King, Bishops and Pawns, and along the second from adverse Knights.

TOPOGRAPHY OF THE BISHOP

From the view-point of the *Bishop*, the surface of the Chess-board takes on a topographical aspect most forbidding.

To this Chess-piece at least one-half of the Topographical Zone is inaccessible, and under any circumstances his movements are limited to the thirty-two squares of his own color.

Thus, the Topographical Horizon of the Bishop takes the form of a broken country, dotted with high hills, deep lakes, impenetrable swamps, and thick woodlands. But between these obstacles thus set about by Nature, run level valleys, varied in extent and easy of access. This fact so modifies this harshest of all sensible horizons as to make the Bishop next in activity to the Rook.

Within its limited sphere of action, the Bishop may move in either one or four directions with a minimum of nine and a maximum of fourteen points open to his occupation. Unimpeded by other corps blocking his route of march, the Bishop may reach any desired point of his own color on the chess board in two moves.

The weakness peculiar to the topographical horizon of the Bishop is its liability to unopposed attack along verticals and horizontals by the hostile King, Queen and Rooks; and along obliques by the hostile Knights.

TOPOGRAPHY OF THE KNIGHT

From the view-point of the *Knight*, the surface of the Chess-board takes on the aspect of a densely wooded and entirely undeveloped country; made up of a profusion of ponds, rivulets, swamps, etc., none of which are impassable although sufficient to impede progress.

Unless interfered with by kindred or hostile corps, or the limitations of the Chess-board, the Knight always may move either in two, four, six, or eight directions. It may reach any desired point in a minimum of one and a maximum of six moves, and may occupy the sixty-four squares of the Chess- board in the same number of marches.

The weakness of the topographical horizon of the Knight lies in the fact that it never commands adjacent points, nor any of those distant, other than the termini of its own obliques. Hence it is open to unopposed attack along verticals and horizontals from the adverse King, Queen and Rooks, and along diagonals from the adverse King, Queen, Bishop and Pawns.

TOPOGRAPHY OF THE PAWN

From the point of view of the *Pawn*, the surface of the Chess-board takes on the topographical aspect of a country which as it is entered, constantly becomes wilder and more rugged.

The march of the Pawn always is along a valley situated between impracticable natural barriers, and the possible movements of the Pawn always decrease as the distance traveled increases.

Unhindered by either kindred or hostile corps, the Pawn may reach any point of junction in the kindred Logistic Horizon, which is contained within its altitude, in a minimum of five and in a maximum of six moves. It may march only in one direction, except in capturing, when it may acquire the option of acting in three directions.

The weakness of the topographical horizon of the Pawn originates in its inability to command the adjacent country. Therefore, it is exposed to unopposed attack along verticals and horizontals by the hostile King, Queen and Rooks; along diagonals by the adverse King, Queen and Bishops, and along obliques by the adverse Knights.

TOPOGRAPHY OF THE TOPOGRAPHICAL ZONE

That normal and visible surface of the *Chess-board* termed the Topographical Zone is bounded by four great natural barriers, impassable to any Chess-piece.

The two sides of the zone may be held to typify either the Ocean or the boundaries of neutral States. The two extremities of the Chess-board while holding the previously announced relation to Chess-pieces contained in the Topographical Zone, also holds another and radically different relation to those Chess-pieces *not* contained in the Topographical Zone, viz.:

In the latter case, the two extremities of the chessboard are to be regarded as two great mountain ranges, each of which is pierced by eight defiles, the latter being the sixteen points of junction contained in the kindred and adverse logistic horizons.

In the arena thus formed by these four great natural barriers, two hostile armies composed of the thirty-two Chess-pieces, are contending for the mastery.

Meanwhile, beyond these great mountain ranges, are advancing to the aid of the combatants, two other armies, represented by the power of promotion possessed by the Pawns. Each of these two hypothetical armies is assailing the outer slope of that range of mountains which lies in the rear of the hostile force. Its effort is to pass one of the eight defiles and by occupying a Point of Junction in the kindred Logistic Horizon, to gain entrance into the Topographical Zone. Then in the array of a Queen, or some other kindred piece, it purposes to attack decisively, the adverse Strategetic Rear.

To oppose the attack of this hypothetical hostile army, whose movements always are typified by the advance of the adverse Pawns, is the duty of the kindred column of manoeuvre.

Primarily this labor falls upon the kindred Pawns. Upon each Pawn devolves the duty of guarding that defile situated directly on its front, by maintaining itself as a Point of Impenetrability between the corresponding hostile pawn and the kindred Strategic Rear.

Conversely, a second duty devolves upon each Pawn; and as an integer of the Column of Support, it continually must threaten and whenever opportunity is presented it decisively must assault the defile on its front, for the purpose of penetrating to the kindred logistic horizon and becoming promoted to such kindred piece, as by attacking the adverse Determinate Force in flank, in rear, or in both, may decide the victory in favor of the kindred army.

Every variety of topography has peculiar requirements for its attack and its defence; and situations even though but little different from each other, nevertheless must be treated according to their particular nature.

In order to acquire the habit of selecting at a glance the correct posts for an army and of making proper dispositions of the kindred corps with rapidity and precision, topography should be studied with great attention, for most frequently it happens that circumstances do not allow time to do these things with deliberation.

PRINCIPLE

Acting either offensively or defensively, one never should proceed in such a
way as to allow the enemy the advantage of ground;

That is to say: Kindred corps never should be exposed to unopposed adverse radii of offence, when the effect of such exposure is the loss of kindred material, or of time much better to be employed, than in making a necessary and servile retreat from an untenable post.

On the contrary, every kindred topographical advantage should unhesitatingly be availed of; and particular attention continually should be paid to advancing the kindred corps to points offensive where they cannot be successfully attacked.

Pains always must be taken to select advantageous ground. Indifferent posts must never be occupied from sheer indolence or from over-confidence in the strength of the kindred, or the weakness of the adverse army.

Particularly must one beware of permitting the enemy to retain advantages in topography; always and at once he should be dislodged from posts whose continued occupation may facilitate his giving an unforeseen and often a fatal blow.

The full importance of topography perhaps is best expressed in the following dictum by the great Frederic:

PRINCIPLE

"Whenever a general and decisive topographical advantage is presented, one has merely to avail of this, without troubling about anything further."

The relative advantage in Topography possessed by one army over an opposing army, always can be determined by the following, viz.:

RULE

1. If the principal adverse Corps of Position are situated upon points of a given color, and if the principal Kindred Corps of Position are situated upon points *not* of the given color, then:

That army which has the *more* Corps of Evolution able to act against points of the given color, and the *equality* in Corps of Evolution able to act against points of the opposite color, has the relative advantage in Topography.

2. To utilize the relative advantage in Topography, construct a position in which the kindred Corps of Position necessary to be defended shall occupy a point upon the sub-geometric symbol of a kindred Corps of Evolution; which point shall be a Tactical Key of a True Strategetic Horizon of which the kindred Corps of Evolution is the Corps of the Centre and of which either the adverse King or an undefendable adverse piece is the second Tactical Key.

3. To neutralize the relative disadvantage in Topography, eliminate that adverse Corps d'armee which is able to act simultaneously by its geometric symbol against the principal Kindred Corps of Position upon a given color; and by its sub-geometric symbol against points of opposite color.

Perfection in Defensive Topography is attained whenever the ground occupied nullifies hostile advantages in Time, Organization, Mobility, Numbers and Position.

Perfection in Offensive Topography is attained whenever the ground occupied accentuates the kindred advantages in Time, Organization, Mobility,

Numbers and Position.

MILITARY EXAMPLES

"When you intend to engage in battle endeavor that your CHIEF advantage shall arise from the ground occupied by your army."— Vegetius.

To cross the Granicus, Alexander the Great selected a fordable spot where the river made a long, narrow bend, and attacked the salient and both sides simultaneously. The Persians thus outflanked were easily and quickly routed; whereupon the Grecian army in line of Phalanxes, both flanks covered by the river and its retreat assured by the fords in rear, advanced to battle in harmony with all requirements of Strategetic Art.

At Issus, Alexander the Great so manoeuvred that the Persian army of more than a million men was confined in a long valley not over three miles in width, having the sea on the left hand and the Amanus Mountains on the right, thus the Grecians had a battlefield fitted to the size of their army, and fought in Phalanxes in line, both wings covered by impassable natural barriers and retreat assured, by open ground in rear.

At the Trebia, Hannibal by stratagems now undiscernible, induced the consul Sempronius to pass the river and following along the easterly bank to take position with his army upon the lowlands between an unfordable part of the stream and the Carthagenians.

Upon this, Hannibal detached his youngest brother Margo to cut off the retreat of the Romans from the ford by which they had crossed the Trebia; advanced his infantry by Phalanxes in line and overthrowing the few Roman horse, assailed the hostile left wing with 10,000 heavy cavalry. The destruction of the Roman army was completed by the simultaneous attack of their right wing by Margo and the impossibility of repassing the river in their rear.

By one of the most notable marches in surprise recorded in military annals, Hannibal crossed the seemingly impassible marshes of the river Po, and turned the left flank of the Roman army, commanded by the Consul C.

Flaminius. Then the great Carthagenian advanced swiftly toward the city of Rome, devasting the country on either hand.

In headlong pursuit the Consul entered a long narrow valley, having Lake Trasymenus on the one hand and the mountains on the other.

Suddenly while entombed in this vast ravine, the Roman army was attacked by infantry from the high ground along its right flank; and in front and rear by the Carthagenian heavy cavalry, while the lake extending along its left flank made futile all attempts to escape.

───────────

At Cannae, Hannibal reproduced the evolutions of Alexander the Great at the passage of the Granicus. Selecting a long bend in the Aufidus, Hannibal forded the river and took position by Phalanxes in line, his flanks covered by unfordable parts of the stream and his retreat assured by the fords by which he had crossed, while as at Issus, the ground on his front though fitting his own army, was so confined as to prevent the Romans engaging a force greater than his own. Beyond Hannibal's front, the hostile army was posted in a wide level plain, suited to the best use of the vastly superior Carthagenian heavy cavalry, both for the evolutions of the battle and the subsequent pursuit and massacre of the Romans.

───────────

At the River Arar (58 B.C.) Caesar achieved his first victory. Following leisurely but closely the marauding Helvetii, he permitted three-fourths of their army to cross to the westerly side of the river; then he fell upon the remainder with his whole army.

───────────

An eye-witness thus describes the famous passage of the Lech by Gustavus Adolphus:

"Resolved to view the situation of the enemy, his majesty went out the 2nd of April (1632) with a strong body of horse, which I had the honor to command. We marched as near as we could to the bank of the river, not to be too much exposed to the enemy's cannon; and having gained a height where the whole course of the river might be seen, we drew up and the king alighted and examined every reach and turning of the river with his glass. Toward the north, he found the river fetching a long reach and doubling short upon itself. 'There is the point will do our business,' says the king, 'and if the ground be good, we will pass there, though Tilly do his worst'."

He immediately ordered a small party of horse to bring him word how high the bank was on each side and at the point, "and he shall have fifty dollars" says the king, "who will tell me how deep the water is."

… The depth and breadths of the stream having been ascertained, and the bank on our side being ten to twelve feet higher than the other and of a hard gravel, the king resolved to cross there; and himself gave directions for such a bridge as I believe never army passed before nor since.

The bridge was loose plank placed upon large tressels as bricklayers raise a scaffold to build a wall. The tressels were made some higher and some lower to answer to the river as it grew deeper or shallower; and all was framed and fitted before any attempt was made to cross.

At night, April 4th the king posted about 2,000 men near the point and ordered them to throw up trenches on either side and quite around it; within which at each end the king placed a battery of six pieces and six cannon at the point, two guns in front and two at each side. By daylight, all the batteries were finished, the trenches filled with musketeers and all the bridge equipment at hand in readiness for use. To conceal this work the king had fired all night at other places along the river.

At daylight, the Imperialists discovered the king's design, when it was too late to prevent it. The musketeers and the batteries made such continual fire that the other bank twelve feet below was too hot for the Imperialists; whereupon old Tilly to be ready for the king on his coming over on his bridge, fell to work and raised a twenty-gun battery right against the point and a breast-work as near the river as he could to cover his men; thinking that when the King should build his bridge, he might easily beat it down with his cannon.

But the King had doubly prevented him; first by laying his bridge so low that none of Tilly's shot could hurt it, for the bridge lay not above half a foot above the water's edge; and the angle of the river secured it against the batteries on the other side, while the continual fire beat the Imperialists from those places where they had no works to cover them.

Now, in the second place, the King sent over four hundred men who cast up a large ravelin on the other bank just where he planned to land; and while this was doing the King laid over his bridge.

71

Both sides wrought hard all the day and all the night as if the spade, not the sword, was to decide the controversy; meanwhile the musketry and cannon-balls flew like hail and both sides had enough to do to make the men stand to their work. The carnage was great; many officers were killed. Both the King and Tilly animated the troops by their presence.

About one o'clock about the time when the King had his bridge finished and in heading a charge of 3000 foot against our ravelin was brave old Tilly slain by a musket bullet in the thigh.

We knew nothing of this disaster befallen them, and the King, who looked for blows, the bridge and ravelin being finished, ordered to run a line of palisades to take in more ground and to cover the first troops he should send over. This work being finished the same night, the King sent over his Guards and six hundred Scots to man the new line.

Early in the morning a party of Scots under Capt. Forbes of Lord Rae's regiment was sent abroad to learn something of the enemy and Sir John Hepburn with the Scots Brigade was ordered to pass the bridge, draw up outside the ravelin, and to advance in search of the enemy as soon as the horse were come over.

The King was by this time at the head of his army in full battle array, ready to follow his van-guard and expecting a hot day's work of it. Sir John sent messenger after messenger entreating for permission to advance, but the King would not suffer it; for he was ever on his guard and would not risk a surprise. So the army continued on this side of the Lech all day and the next night.

In the morning the King ordered 300 horse, 600 horse and 800 dragoons to enter the wood by three ways, but sustaining each other; the Scots Brigade to follow to the edge of the wood in support of all, and a brigade of Swedish infantry to cover Sir John's troops. So warily did this famous warrior proceed.

The next day the cavalry came up with us led by Gustavus Horn; and the King and the whole army followed, and we marched on through the heart of Bavaria. His Majesty when he saw the judgment with which old Tilly had prepared his works and the dangers we had run, would often say, "That day's work is every way equal to the victory of Leipsic."

With but 55,000 troops in hand and surrounded by the united Austrian and Russian armies aggregating a quarter of a million men; Frederic the Great availing of a swamp, a few hills, a rivulet and a fortified town, constructed a battlefield upon which his opponents dared not engage him.

This famous camp of Bunzlewitz is one of the wonders of the military art. It also is an illustration of the inability of the Anglo-Saxon to reason; for to this day many who wear epaulets, accepting the dictum of a skillfully hoodwinked French diplomat at the siege of Neisse, (Dec., 1740) commonly assert that "the great Frederic was a bad engineer."

Washington compelled the British to evacuate Boston, merely by occupying with artillery Dorchester Heights, the tactical key of the theatre of action and thus preventing either ingress or egress from the harbor.

At Trenton the Hessian column was unable to escape from Washington's accurate evolutions, on account of being imprisoned in an angle formed by the unfordable Delaware river.

At Yorktown, the British army under Lord Cornwallis was captured entire, being cut off from all retreat by the ocean on the right flank and the James river in rear.

Bonaparte made his reputation at Toulon (1793) merely by following the method employed by Washington in the siege of Boston.

Bonaparte gained his first success in Italy because the allied Piedmontese and Austrian armies, although thrice his numbers, were separated by the Apennine mountains.

Bonaparte's success at Castiglione was due to the separation of the Austrian army into two great isolated columns by the Lake of Garda.

At Arcola, Bonaparte occupied a great swamp upon the hostile strategic center and the Austrian army was destroyed by its efforts to dislodge him.

At Rivoli, the Austrian army purposed to unite its five detached wings upon a plateau of which Bonaparte was already in possession. All were ruined in the effort to dislodge the French from this Tactical Center.

The Austrian army was unable to escape after Marengo on account of the Po river in its rear.

At Austerlitz the left wing of the Austro-Russian army was caught between the French army and a chain of lakes and rivulets and totally destroyed.

At Friedland the Russian army was caught between the French in front and the Vistula river in rear and totally destroyed.

At Krasnoe, the Russians under Kutosof, occupied the strategic center and were covered by the Dnieper. To force the passage of the river cost Napoleon 30,000 men.

At the Beresina, the Russians under Benningsen, occupied the Strategic Center and were covered by the unfordable river. To force the passage cost Napoleon 20,000 men.

––––––––

At Leipsic, Napoleon was caught between the allied army and the Elbe. The retreat across the river cost the French 50,000 men.

––––––––

At Waterloo, the high plateau sloping gradually to a plain, various hamlets on front and flank and the forest in rear, made a perfect topography for a defensive battle.

––––––––

At Sedan, the Emperor, Napoleon III, and his army were enclosed between the Prussian army and the frontier of Belgium and captured.

––––––––

"Where the real general incessantly sees prepared by Nature means admirably adapted for his needs, the commander lacking such talents sees nothing."—Hannibal.

––––––––

MOBILITY

"Success in an operation depends upon the secrecy and celerity with which the movements are made."—Napoleon.

"An eye unskilled and a mind untutored can see but little where a trained observer detects important movements."—Von Moltke.

"Caesar is a marvel of vigilance and rapidity, he finishes a war in a march."—Cicero.

MOBILITY

"Victory lies in the legs of the soldier."—Frederic the Great.

"The principal part of the soldier's efficiency depends upon his legs.

"The personal abilities required in all manoeuvres and in battles are totally confined to them.

"Whoever is of a different opinion is a dupe to ignorance and a novice in the profession of arms."—Count de Saxe.

"It is easier to beat an enemy than commonly is supposed," says Napoleon, "the great Art lies in making nothing but decisive movements."

To the proficient in Strategetics the truth of the foregoing dictum is self-evident. Nevertheless, it remains to instruct the student how to select from a multitude of possible movements, that particular movement or series of movements, which in a given situation are best calculated to achieve victory.

Whatever may be such series of movements, obviously, it must have an object, *i.e.*, a specific and clearly defined purpose. Equally so, all movements made on such line of movement must each have an objective, *i.e.*, a terminus. These objectives, like cogs in a gear, intimately are connected with other objectives or termini, so that the project thus formed constitutes always an exact and often a vast scheme.

Frequently it happens that the occupation of an objective, valid in a given situation, is not valid in an ensuing situation for the reasons:

1. That the object of the given line of movement is become unattainable, or,

2. Because it has become no longer worth attaining, or,

3. Because such belated attainment may be direct cause of disaster.

PRINCIPLE

In order to select the decisive movement in a given situation it is necessary first to determine both the object and the objective, not merely of the required movement, but also of that series of movements, which collectively constitute the projected line of movement; together with the object and the objective of every movement contained therein.

The mathematician readily will perceive, and the student doubtless will permit himself to be informed, that:

Before the true object and the true objective of any movement can be determined it first is necessary to deduce the common object of all movement.

―――――――

As is well known, the combined movements of the Chess-pieces over the surface of the Chess-board during a game at Chess are infinite.

These calculations are so complex that human perception accurately can forecast ultimate and even immediate results only in comparatively few and simple situations. Such calculable outcomes are limited to the earlier stages of the opening, to the concluding phases of a game; and to situations in the mid-game wherein the presence of but few adverse pieces minimizes the volume of effort possible to the opponent.

Consequently, it is self-evident, that:

PRINCIPLE

Situations on the Chess-board require for their demonstration a degree of skill which decreases as the hostile power of resistance decreases.

All power for resistance possessed by an army emanates from its ability to move. This faculty of Mobility is that inestimable quality without which nothing and by means of which everything, can be done.

From this truth it is easy to deduce the common object of all movement, which obviously is:

To minimize the mobility of the opposing force.

The hostile army having the ability to move and consequently a power for resistance equal to that possessed by the kindred army; it becomes of the first importance to discover in what way the kindred army is superior to that adverse force, which in the Normal Situation on the Chess-board is its exact counterpart in material, position and formation.

Such normal superiority of the White army over the Black army is found in the fact that:

1. The former has the privilege of making the initial move of the game.

2. This privilege of first move is the absolute advantage in Time.

While no mathematical demonstration of the outcome of a game at Chess is possible, nevertheless there are rational grounds for assuming that with exact play, White should win.

This decided and probably decisive advantage possessed by White can be minimized only by correcting a mathematical blemish in the game of Chess as at present constructed; which blemish, there is reason to believe, did not originally exist.

This imperfection seemingly is the result of unscientific modifications of the Italian method of Castling; which latter, from the standpoint of mathematics and of Strategetics, embodies the true spirit of that delicate and vital evolution.

To the mathematician and to the Strategist, it is clear that Chess as first devised was geometrically perfect. The abortions played during successive ages and in various parts of the Earth, merely are crude and unscientific deviations from the perfect original.

Thus, strategetically, the correct post of deployment for the Chess-King is at the extremity of a straight line drawn from the center of that Grand Strategic Front which appertains to the existing formation.

Hence, in the grand front by the right, the King in Castling K R, properly goes in one move to KKt1, his proper post. Conversely, in Castling Q R, he also should go in one move to QKt1, his proper post corresponding to the grand front by the left.

Again, whenever the formation logically points to the grand front by the right refused, the King should go in one move from K1 to KR1. When the formations indicate the grand front by the left refused, the King should go in one move from K1 to QR1.

In each and every case the co-operating Rook should be posted at the corresponding Bishop's square, in order to support the alignment by P-B4, of the front adopted.

The faulty mode of castling today in vogue clearly is not the product either of the mathematic nor of the strategetic mind.

The infantile definition of "the books," viz., "The King in Castling moves two squares either to the right or to the left," displays all that mania for the commonplace, which characterizes the dilettante.

All that can be done is to call attention to this baleful excrescence on the great Game. Of course, it is useless to combat it. In the words of the Count de Saxe:

> "The power of custom is absolute. To depart from it is a crime, and the most inexcusable of all crimes is to introduce innovations. For most people, it is sufficient that a thing is so, to forever allow it to remain so."

Says the great Frederic;

> "Man hardly may eradicate in his short lifetime all the prejudices that are imbibed with his mother's milk; and it is well nigh impossible to successfully wrestle with custom, that chief argument of fools."

Also bearing in mind the irony of Cicero, who regarded himself fortunate in that he had not fallen victim to services rendered his countrymen, it suffices to say:

The true Chessic dictum in regard to the double evolution of the King and Rook should read:

> *"The King of Castling should deploy in one move to that point where, as the Base of Operations, it mathematically harmonizes with that Strategic Front, which is, or must become, established."*

The change in the present form of Castling, herein suggested, should be made in the true interests of the Royal Game.

The instant effect of such change will be:

1. Largely to increase the defensive resources both of White and Black;

2. To minimize the handicap on the second player, due to White's advantage of first move;

3. To permit open play on the Queen's side of the board and thus provide a broader and more resplendent field for Strategetic genius.

In all our modern-day mis-interpretations of the ethics of Chess and our characteristic Twentieth Century looseness of practice as applied to Chess-play, perhaps there exists no greater absurdity, than that subversion of ordinary intelligence, daily evinced by permitting a piece which cannot move, to give check.

It is a well known and in many ways a deserved reproach, cast by the German erudite, that the mind of the Anglo-Saxon is not properly developed, that it is able to act correctly only when dealing with known quantities, and is inadequate for the elucidation of indeterminate things.

In consequence, they say, the argumentative attempts of the Anglo-Saxon are puerile; the natural result of a mental limitation which differs from that of monkeys and parrots, merely in ability to count beyond two.

Surely it would seem that a very young child readily would sense that:

A Chess-piece, which by law is debarred from movement, is, by the same law, necessarily debarred from capturing adverse material; inasmuch as in order to capture, a piece must move.

Nevertheless consensus of opinion today among children of every growth and whether Anglo-Saxon or German, universally countenance the paradox that:

A piece which is pinned on its own King, can give check *i.e.*, threaten to move and capture the adverse King.

To argue this question correctly and to deduce the logical solution, it is necessary to revert to first principles and to note that:

It is a fundamental of Chess mathematics that the King cannot be exposed to capture.

Furthermore, it is to be noted as equally fundamental, that:

1. A piece exerts no force against that point upon which it is posted;
2. That whatever power a piece exerts, always is exerted against some other point than the point upon which it stands; and that;
3. In order to exert such power, it is an all-essential that the piece move from the point which it occupies to the point at which its power is to be exerted.

Hence, it is obvious and may be mathematically demonstrated, that,

1. A piece which cannot move, cannot capture.
2. A piece which cannot capture, does not exercise any threat of capture; and
3. Consequently, a piece deprived of its right to move; which cannot capture nor exercise any threat to capture, obviously and by mathematical demonstration, cannot give check, inasmuch, as

"check" merely is the threat by a piece to move and capture the adverse King.

Therefore, whatever may be the normal area of movement belonging to a piece, whenever from any cause such piece loses its power of movement, then,

It no longer can capture, nor exercise any threat of capture, upon the points contained within said area; and consequently such points so far as said immovable piece is concerned, may be occupied in safety by any adverse piece including the adverse King, for the reason that:

An immovable piece cannot move; and not being able to move it cannot capture, and not being able to capture, it does not exercise any threat of capture, and consequently it cannot give check.

This incongruity of permitting an immovable piece to give check constitutes the second mathematical blemish in the game of Chess, as at present constructed.

This fallacy, the correction of which any schoolboy may mathematically demonstrate, is defended, even by many who would know better, if they merely would take time for reflection; by the inane assumption, that:

A piece which admittedly is disqualified and rendered dormant by all the fundamentals of the science of Chess, and which therefore cannot legally move and consequently cannot legally capture anything; by some hocus- pocus may be made to move and to capture that *most* valuable of *all* prizes, the adverse King; and this at a time and under circumstances when, as is universally allowed, it cannot legally move against, nor legally capture *any other* adverse piece.

The basis of this illogical, illegal, and untenable assumption is:

The pinned piece, belonging to that force which has the privilege of moving, can abandon its post, and capture the adverse King; this stroke ends the game and the game being ended, the pinning piece never can avail of the abandonment of the covering post by the pinned piece to capture the King thus exposed.

The insufficiency of this subterfuge is clear to the mathematical mind. Its subtlety lies in confounding together things which have no connection, viz.:

Admittedly the given body of Chess-pieces has the right to move, but it is of the utmost importance to note that this privilege of moving extends only to a single piece and from this privilege of moving the pinned piece is debarred by a specific and fundamental law of the game, which declares that:

"A piece shall not by removing itself uncover the kindred King to the attack of a hostile piece."

Thus, it is clear, that a pinned piece is a disqualified piece; its powers are dormant and by the laws of the game it is temporarily reduced to an inert mass, and deprived of every faculty normally appertaining to it as a Chess- piece. On the other hand, as is equally obvious, the pinning piece is in full possession of its normal powers and is qualified to perform every function.

To hold that a piece disqualified by the laws of the game can nullify the activities of a piece in full possession of its powers, is to assert that black is white, that the moon is made of green cheese, that the tail can wag the dog, or any other of those things which have led the German to promulgate his caustic formula on the Anglo-Saxon.

Hence, artificially to nullify the normal powers of an active and potential piece which is operating in conformity to the laws of the game, and artificially to revivify the dormant powers of a piece disqualified by the same laws; to debar the former from exercising its legitimate functions and to permit the latter to exercise functions from which by law, it specifically is debarred, is a self-evident incongruity and any argument whereby such procedure is upheld, necessarily and obviously, is sophistry.

———

No less interesting than instructive and conclusive, is reference of this question to those intellectual principles which give birth to the game of Chess, *per se*, viz.:

As a primary fundamental, with the power to give check, is associated concurrently the obligation upon the King thus checked, not to remain in check.

Secondly: The totality of powers assigned to the Chess-pieces is the ability to move, provided the King be free from check. This totality of powers may be denoted by the indefinite symbol, X.

The play thus has for its object:

The reduction to zero of the adverse X, by the operation of the kindred X.

This result is checkmate in its generalized form. In effect, it is the destruction of the power of the adverse pieces to move, by means of check made permanent.

By the law of continuity it is self-evident that:

The power to move appertaining either to White or to Black, runs from full power to move any piece (a power due to freedom from check), down to total inability to move any piece, due to his King being permanently checked, *i.e.*, checkmated.

This series cannot be interrupted without obvious violation of the ethics of the game; because, so long as any part of X remains, the principle from which the series emanated still operates, and this without regard to quantity of X remaining unexpended.

Thus, a game of Chess is a procedure from total ability to total disability; *i.e.*, from one logical whole to another; otherwise, from X to zero.

Checkmate, furnishes the limit to the series; the game and X vanish together.

This is in perfect keeping with the law of continuity, which acts and dominates from beginning to end of the series, and so long as any part of X remains.

Hence to permit either White or Black to move any piece, leaving his King in check, is an anomaly.

Denial to the Pawn of ability to move to the rear is an accurate interpretation of military ethics.

Of those puerile hypotheses common to the man who does not know, one of the most entrancing to the popular mind, is the notion that Corps d'armee properly are of equal numbers and of the same composition.

This supposition is due to ignorance of the fact that the multifarious duties of applied Strategetics, require for their execution like variety of instruments, which diversity of means is strikingly illustrated by the differing movements of the Chess-pieces.

The inability of the Pawn to move backward strategically harmonizes with its functions as a Corps of Position, in contradiction to the movements of the pieces, which latter are Corps of Evolution.

This restriction in the move of the Pawn is in exact harmony with the inability of the Queen to move on obliques, of the Rook to move on obliques or on diagonals, of the Bishop to move on obliques, verticals and horizontals, of the Knight to move on diagonals, verticals, and horizontals, and of the King to move like any other piece.

Possessed of the invaluable privilege of making the first move in the game, knowing that no move should be made without an object, understanding that the true object of every move is to minimize the adverse power for resistance and comprehending that all power for resistance is derived from facility of movement, the student easily deduces the true object of White's initial move in every game of Chess, viz.:

PRINCIPLE

To make the first of a series of movements, each of which shall increase the mobility of the kindred pieces and correspondingly decrease the mobility of the adverse pieces.

As the effect of such policy, the power for resistance appertaining to Black, ultimately must become so insufficient that he no longer will be able adequately to defend:

1. His base of operations.

2. The communications of his army with its base.

3. The communications of his corps d'armee with each other, or,

4. To prevent the White hypothetical force penetrating to its Logistic Horizon.

To produce this fatal weakness in the Black position by the advantage of the first move is much easier for White than commonly is supposed.

The process consists in making only those movements by means of which the kindred corps d'armee, progressively occupying specified objectives, are advanced, viz.:

I. To the Strategetic Objective, when acting against the communications of the adverse Determinate Force and its Base of Operations.

II. To the Logistic Horizon, when acting against the communications between the adverse Determinate and the adverse Hypothetical Forces.

III. To the Strategic Vertices, when acting against the communications of the hostile corps d'armee with each other.

To bring about either of these results against an opponent equally equipped and capable, of course is a much more difficult task than to checkmate an enemy incapable of movement.

Yet such achievement is possible to White and with exact play it seemingly is a certainty that he succeeds in one or the other, owing to his inestimable privilege of first move.

For the normal advantage that attaches to the first move in a game of Chess is vastly enhanced by a peculiarity in the mathematical make-up of the surface of the Chess-board, whereby, he who makes the first move may secure to himself the advantage in mobility, and conversely may inflict upon the second player a corresponding disadvantage in mobility.

This peculiar property emanates from this fact:

> *The sixty-four points, i.e., the sixty-four centres of the squares into which the surface of the Chess-board is divided, constitute, when taken collectively, the quadrant of a circle, whose radius is eight points in length.*

Hence, in Chessic mathematics, the sides of the Chessboard do not form a square, but the segment of a circumference.

To prove the truth of this, one has but to count the points contained in the verticals and horizontals and in the hypothenuse of each corresponding angle, and in every instance it will be found that the number of points contained in the base, perpendicular, and hypothenuse, is the same.

For example:

Let the eight points of the King's Rook's file form the perpendicular of a right angle triangle, of which the kindred first horizontal forms the base; then, the hypothenuse of the given angle, will be that diagonal which extends from QR1 to KR8. Now, merely by the processes of simple arithmetic, it may be shown that there are,

1. Eight points in the base.

2. Eight points in the perpendicular.

3. Eight points in the hypothenuse.

Consequently the *three* sides of this given right angled triangle are *equal* to each other, which is a geometric *impossibility*.

Therefore, it is self-evident that there exists a mathematical incongruity in the surface of the Chess-board.

That is, what to the eye *seems* a right angled triangle, is in its relations to the *movements* of the Chess-pieces, an equilateral triangle. Hence, the Chess-board, in its relations to the pieces when the latter are at *rest*, properly may be regarded as a great *square* sub-divided into sixty-four smaller squares; but on the contrary, in those calculations relating to the Chess-pieces in *motion*, the Chess-board must be regarded as the *quadrant* of a circle of eight points radius. The demonstration follows, viz.:

Connect by a straight line the points KR8 and QR8. Connect by another straight line the points QR8 and QR1. Connect each of the fifteen points through which these lines pass with the point KR1, by means of lines passing through the least number of points intervening.

Then the line KR8 and QR8 will represent the segment of a circle of which latter the point KR1 is the center. The lines KR1-KR8 and KR1-QR1 will represent the sides of a quadrant contained in the given circle and bounded by the given segment, and the lines drawn from KR1 to the fifteen points contained in the given segment of the given circumference, will be found to be fifteen equal radii each eight points in length.

Having noted the form of the Static or positional surface of the Chess-board and its relations to the pieces at rest, and having established the configuration of the Dynamic surface upon which the pieces move, it is next in sequence to deduce that fundamental fact and to give it that geometric expression which shall mathematically harmonize these conflicting geometric figures in their relations to Chess-play.

As the basic fact of applied Chessic forces, it is to be noted, that:

PRINCIPLE

The King is the SOURCE from whence the Chess-pieces derive all power of movement; and from his ability to move, emanates ALL power for attack and for defence possessed by a Chessic army.

This faculty of mobility, derived from the existence of the kindred King, is the all essential element in Chess-play, and to increase the mobility of the kindred pieces and to reduce that of the adverse pieces is the simple, sure and only scientific road to victory; and by comparison of the Static with the Dynamic surface of the Chess-board, the desired principle readily is discovered, viz.,

The Static surface of the Chess-board being a square, its least division is into two great right angled triangles having a common hypothenuse.

The Dynamic surface being the quadrant of a circle, its least division also is into two great sections, one of which is a right angled triangle and the other a semi-circle.

Comparing the two surfaces of the Chess-board thus divided, it will be seen that these three great right angled triangles are equal, each containing thirty-six points; and having for their common vertices, the points KR1, QR1 and R8.

Furthermore, it will be seen that the hypothenuse common to these triangles, also is the chord of that semi-circle which appertains to the Dynamic surface.

Again, it will be perceived that this semi-circle, like the three right angled triangles, is composed of thirty-six points, and consequently that all of the four sub-divisions of the Static and Dynamic surfaces of the Chess-board are equal.

Thus it obviously follows, that:

1. The great central diagonal, always is one side of each of the four chief geometric figures into which the Chess board is divided; that:

2. It mathematically perfects each of these figures and harmonizes each to all, and that:

3. By means of it each figure becomes possessed of eight more points than it otherwise would contain.

Hence, the following is self-evident:

PRINCIPLE

That Chessic army which can possess itself of the great central diagonal, thereby acquires the larger number of points upon which to act and consequently greater facilities for movement; and conversely:

By the loss of the great central diagonal, the mobility of the opposing army is correspondingly decreased.

It therefore is clear that the object of any series of movements by a Chessic army acting otherwise than on Line of Operations, should be:

PRINCIPLE

Form the kindred army upon the hypothenuse of the right angled triangle which is contained within the Dynamic surface of the Chess-board; and conversely,

Compel the adverse army to act exclusively within that semi-circle which appertains to the same surface.

Under these circumstances, the kindred corps will be possessed of facilities for movement represented by thirty-six squares; while the logistic area of the opposing army will be restricted to twenty-eight squares.

There are, of course, two great central diagonals of the Chess-board; but as the student is fully informed that great central diagonal always is to be selected, which extends towards the Objective Plane.

————————————

Mobility, *per se*, increases or decreases with the number of squares open to occupation.

But in all situations there will be points of no value, while other points are of value inestimable; for the reason that the occupation of the former will not favorably affect the play, or may even lose the game; while by the occupation of the latter, victory is at once secured.

But it is not the province of Mobility to pass on the values of points; this latter is the duty of Strategy. It is sufficient for Mobility that it provide superior facilities for movement; it is for Strategy to define the Line of Movement; for Logistics, by means of this Line of Movement, to bring into action in proper times and sequence, the required force, and for Tactics, with this force, to execute the proper evolutions.

Mobility derives its importance from three things which may occur severally or in combination, viz.:

1. All power for offense or for defense is eliminated from a Chess-piece the instant it loses its ability to move.

2. The superiority possessed by corps acting offensively over adverse corps acting defensively, resides in that the attack of a piece is valid at every point which it menaces; while the defensive effort of a piece, as a rule, is valid only at a single point. Consequently:

PRINCIPLE

Increased facilities for movement enhance the power of attacking pieces in a much greater degree than like facilities enhance the power of defending pieces.

Such increasing facilities for movement ultimately render an attacking force irresistible, for the reason that it finally becomes a physical impossibility for the opposing equal force to provide valid defences for the numerous tactical keys, which at a given time become simultaneously assailed. Hence:

PRINCIPLE

Superior facilities for occupying any point at any time and with any force, always ensure the superior force at a given point, at a given time.

The relative advantage in mobility possessed by one army over an opposing army always can be determined by the following, viz.:

RULE

1. That army whose strategic front of operations is established upon the Strategetic Center has the relative advantage in Mobility.
2. To utilize the advantage in Mobility extend the Strategic Front in the direction of the objective plane.
3. To neutralize the relative disadvantage in Mobility eliminate that adverse Corps d'armee which tactically expresses such adverse advantage; or so post the Prime Strategetic Point as to vitiate the adverse Strategic front.

Advantage in Mobility is divided into two classes, viz.:

I. General Advantage in Mobility.

II. Special Advantage in Mobility.

A General Advantage in Mobility consists in the ability to act simultaneously against two or more vital points by means of interior logistic radii due to position between:—

1. The adverse army and its Base of Operations.

2. Two or more adverse Grand Columns.

3. The wings of a hostile Grand Column.

4. Two or more isolated adverse Corps d'armee.

Such position upon interior lines of movement is secured by occupying either of the Prime Offensive Origins, *i.e.*:

1. Strategic Center *vs.* Adverse Formation in Mass.

2. Logistic Center *vs.* Adverse Formation by Grand Columns.

3. Tactical Center *vs.* Adverse Formation by Wings.

4. Logistic Triune *vs.* Adverse Formation by Corps.

Special Advantage in Mobility consists in the ability of a corps d'armee to traverse greater or equal distances in lesser times than opposing corps.

MILITARY EXAMPLES

"Never interrupt your enemy when he is making a false movement."—Napoleon.

In the year (366 B.C.) the King of Sparta, with an army of 30,000 men marched to the aid of the Mantineans against Thebes. Epaminondas took up a post with his army from whence he equally threatened Mantinea and Sparta. Agesilaus incautiously moved too far towards the coast, whereupon Epaminondas, with 70,000 men precipitated himself upon Lacedaemonia, laying waste the country with fire and sword, all but taking by storm the city of Sparta and showing the women of Lacedaemonia the campfire of an enemy for the first time in six hundred years.

———

Flaminius advancing incautiously to oppose Hannibal, the latter took up a post with his army from whence he equally threatened the city of Rome and the army of the Consul. In the endeavor to rectify his error, the Roman general committed a worse and was destroyed with his entire army.

———

At Thapsus, April 6, 46 B.C., Caesar took up a post with his army from whence he equally threatened the Roman army under Scipio and the African army under Juba. Scipio having marched off with his troops to a better camp some miles distant, Caesar attacked and annihilated Juba's army.

———

At Pirna, Frederic the Great, captured the Saxon army entire, and at Rossbach, Leuthern and Zorndorf destroyed successively a French, an Austrian and a Russian army merely by occupying a post from whence he equally threatened two or more vital points, awaiting the time when one would become inadequately defended.

———

Washington won the Revolutionary War merely by occupying a post from whence he equally threatened the British armies at New York and Philadelphia; refusing battle and building up an army of Continental regular troops enlisted for the war and trained by the Baron von Steuben in the system of Frederic the Great.

———

Bonaparte won at Montenotte, Castiglione, Arcola, Rivoli and Austerlitz his most perfect exhibitions of generalship, merely by passively threatening two vital points and in his own words: "By never interrupting an enemy when he is making a false movement."

———

Perfection in Mobility is attained whenever the kindred army is able to act unrestrainedly in any and all directions, while the movements of the hostile army are restricted.

———

NUMBERS

"In warfare the advantage in numbers never is to be despised."— Von Moltke.

"Arguments avail but little against him whose opinion is voiced by thirty legions."—Roman Proverb.

"That king who has the most iron is master of those who merely have the more gold."—Solon.

"It never troubles the wolf how many sheep there are."—Agesilaus.

NUMBERS

"A handful of troops inured to Warfare proceed to certain victory; while on the contrary, numerous hordes of raw and undisciplined men are but a multitude of victims dragged to slaughter."—Vegetius.

"Turenne always was victorious with armies infinitely inferior in numbers to those of his enemies; because he moved with expedition, knew how to secure himself from being attacked in every situation and always kept near his enemy."—Count de Saxe.

"Numbers are of no significance when troops are once thrown into confusion."—Prince Eugene.

Humanity is divisible into two groups, one of which relatively is small and the other, by comparison, very large.

The first of these groups is made up comparatively of but a few persons, who, by virtue of circumstances are possessed of everything except adequate physical strength; and the second group consists of those vast multitudes of mankind, which are destitute of everything except of incalculable prowess, due to their overwhelming numbers.

Hence, at every moment of its existence, organized Society is face to face with the possibility of collision into the Under World; and because of the knowledge that such encounter is inevitable, unforeseeable and perhaps immediately impending, Civilization, so-called, ever is beset by an unspeakable and all-corroding fear.

To deter a multitude, destitute of everything except the power to take, from despoiling by means of its irresistible physique, those few who are possessed of everything except ability to defend themselves, in all Ages has been the chiefest problem of mankind; and to the solution of this problem has been devoted every resource known to Education, Legislation, Ecclesiasticism and Jurisprudence.

This condition further is complicated by a peculiar outgrowth of necessary expedients, always more or less unstable, due to that falsity of premise in which words do not agree with acts.

Of these expedients the most incongruous is the arming and training of the children of the mob for the protection of the upper stratum; and that peculiar mental insufficiency of hoi polloi, whereby it ever is induced to accept as its leaders the sons of the Patrician class.

That a social structure founded upon such anomalies should endure, constitutes in itself the real Nine Wonders of the World; and is proof of that marvellous ingenuity with which the House of Have profits by the chronic predeliction of the House of Want to fritter away time and opportunity, feeding on vain hope.

The advantage in Numbers consists in having in the aggregate more Corps d'armee than has the adversary.

All benefit to be derived from the advantage in Numbers is limited to the active and scientific use of every corp d'armee; otherwise excess of Numbers, not only is of no avail, but easily may degenerate into fatal disadvantage by impeding the decisive action of other kindred corps. Says Napoleon: "It is only the troops brought into action, that avails in battles and campaigns—the rest does not count."

A loss in Numbers at chess-play occurs only when two pieces are lost for one, or three for two, or one for none, and the like. No diminution in aggregate of force can take place on the Chess-board, so long as the number of the opposing pieces are equal.

This is true although all the pieces on one side are Queens and those of the other side all Pawns.

The reason for this is:

All the Chess-pieces are equal in strength, one to the other. The Pawn can overthrow and capture any piece—the Queen can do no more.

That is to say, at its turn to move, any piece can capture any adverse piece; and this is all that any piece can do.

It is true that the Queen, on its turn to move, has a maximum option of twenty-seven squares, while the Pawn's maximum never is more than three. But as the power of the Queen can be exerted only upon one point, obviously, her observation of the remaining twenty-six points is merely a manifestation of mobility, and her display of force is limited to a single square. Hence, the result in each case is identical, and the display of force equal.

The relative advantage in Numbers possessed by one army over an opposing army always can be determined by the following, viz.:

RULE

That army which contains more Corps d'armee than an opposing army has the relative advantage in Numbers.

———————

"With the inferiority in Numbers, one must depend more upon conduct and contrivance than upon strength."—Caesar.

———————

MILITARY EXAMPLES

"He who has the advantage in Numbers, if he be not a blockhead, incessantly will distract his enemy by detachments, against all of which it is impossible to provide a remedy."—Frederic the Great.

"He that hath the advantage in Numbers usually should exchange pieces freely, because the fewer that remain the more readily are they oppressed by a superior force."—Dal Rio.

At Thymbra, Cyrus the Great, king of the Medes and Persians, with 10,000 horse cuirassiers, 20,000 heavy infantry, 300 chariots and 166,000 light troops, conquered Croesus, King of Assyria whose army consisted of 360,000 infantry and 60,000 cavalry. This victory made Persia dominant in Asia.

———————

At Marathon, 10,000 Athenian and 1,000 Plataean heavy infantry, routed 110,000 Medes and Persians. This victory averted the overthrow of Grecian civilization by Asiatic barbarism.

———————

At Leuctra, Epaminondas, general of the Thebans, with 6000 heavy infantry and 400 heavy horse, routed the Lacedaemonean army, composed of 22,000 of the bravest and most skillful soldiers of the known world, and extinguished the military ascendency which for centuries Sparta had exercised over the Grecian commonwealths.

At Issus, Alexander the Great with 40,000 heavy infantry and 7,000 heavy cavalry destroyed the army of Darius Codomannus, King of Persia, which consisted of 1,000,000 infantry, 40,000 cavalry, 200 chariots and 15 elephants. This battle, in which white men encountered elephants for the first time, established the military supremacy of Europe over Asia.

Alexander the Great invaded Asia (May, 334 B.C.) whose armies aggregated 3,000,000 men trained to war; with 30,000 heavy infantry, 4000 heavy cavalry, $225,000 dollars in money and thirty days' provisions.

At Arbela, Alexander the Great with 45,000 heavy infantry and 8,000 heavy horse, annihilated the last resources of Darius and reduced Persia to a Greek province. The Persian army consisted of about 600,000 infantry and cavalry, of whom 300,000 were killed.

Hannibal began his march from Spain (218 B.C.) to invade the Roman commonwealth, with 90,000 heavy infantry and 12,000 heavy cavalry. He arrived at Aosta in October (218 B.C.) with only 20,000 infantry and 6,000 cavalry to encounter a State that could put into the field 700,000 of the bravest and most skillful soldiers then alive.

At Cannae, Hannibal destroyed the finest army Rome ever put in the field. Out of 90,000 of the flower of the commonwealth only about 3,000 escaped. The Carthagenian army consisted of 40,000 heavy infantry and 10,000 heavy cavalry.

At Alesia, (51 B.C.) Caesar completed the subjugation of Gaul, by destroying in detail two hostile armies aggregating 470,000 men. The Roman army consisted of 43,000 heavy infantry, 10,000 heavy cavalry and 10,000 light cavalry.

———

At Pharsaleus, (48 B.C.) Caesar with 22,000 Roman veterans routed 45,000 soldiers under Pompey and acquired the chief place in the Roman state.

———

At Angora, (1402) Tamerlane, with 1,400,000 Asiatics, destroyed the Turkish army of 900,000 men, commanded by the Ottoman Sultan Bajazet, in the most stupendous battle of authentic record.

After giving his final instructions to his officers, Tamerlane, it is recorded, betook himself to his tent and played at Chess until the crisis of the battle arrived, whereupon he proceeded to the decisive point and in person directed those evolutions which resulted in the destruction of the Ottoman army.

The assumption that the great Asiatic warrior was playing at Chess during the earlier part of the battle of Angora, undoubtedly is erroneous. Most probably he followed the progress of the conflict by posting chess-pieces upon the Chessboard and moving these according to reports sent him momentarily by his lieutenants.

Obviously, in the days when the field telegraphy and telephone were unknown, such method was entirely feasible and satisfactory to the Master of Strategetics and far superior to any attempt to overlook such a confused and complicated concourse.

———

At Bannockburne (June 24, 1314), Robert Bruce, King of Scotland, with 30,000 Scots annihilated the largest army that England ever put upon a battlefield.

This army was led by Edward II and consisted of over 100,000 of the flower of England's nobility, gentry and yeomanry. The victory established the independence of Scotland and cost England 30,000 troops, which could not be replaced in that generation.

———

Gustavus Adolphus invaded Germany with an army of 27,000 men, over one-half of whom were Scots and English. At that time the Catholic armies in the field aggregated several hundred thousand trained and hardened soldiers, led by brave and able generals.

At Leipsic, after 20,000 Saxon allies had fled from the battlefield, Gustavus Adolphus with 22,000 Swedes, Scots and English routed 44,000 of the best troops of the day, commanded by Gen. Tilly. This victory delivered the Protestant princes of Continental Europe from Catholic domination.

At Zentha (Sept. 11, 1697), Prince Eugene with 60,000 Austrians routed 150,000 Turks, commanded by the Sultan Kara-Mustapha, with the loss of 38,000 killed, 4,000 prisoners and 160 cannon. This victory established the military reputation of this celebrated French General.

At Turin (Sept. 7, 1706) Prince Eugene with 30,000 Austrians routed 80,000 French under the Duke of Orleans. Gen. Daun, whose brilliant evolutions decided the battle, afterward, as Field-Marshal of the Austrian armies, was routed by Frederic the Great at Leuthern.

At Peterwaradin (Aug. 5, 1716) Prince Eugene with 60,000 Austrians destroyed 150,000 Turks. This victory delivered Europe for all time from the menace of Mahometan dominion.

At Belgrade (Aug. 26, 1717) Prince Eugene with 55,000 Austrians destroyed a Turkish army of 200,000 men.

At Rosbach (Nov. 5, 1757) Frederic the Great with 22,000 Prussians, in open field, destroyed a French army of 70,000 regulars commanded by the

Prince de Soubisse.

At Leuthern (Dec. 5, 1757) Frederic the Great with 33,000 Prussians destroyed in open field, an Austrian army of 93,000 regulars, commanded by Field-Marshal Daun. The Austrians lost 54,000 men and 200 cannon.

At Zorndorf (Aug. 25, 1758) Frederic the Great with 45,000 Prussians destroyed a Russian army of 60,000 men commanded by Field-Marshal Fermor. The Russians left 18,000 men dead on the field.

At Leignitz (Aug. 15, 1760) Frederic the Great with 30,000 men out-manoeuvred, defeated with the loss of 10,000 men and escaped from the combined Austrian and Russian armies aggregating 130,000 men.

At Torgau (Nov. 5, 1760) Frederic the Great with 45,000 Prussians destroyed an Austrian army of 90,000 men, commanded by Field-Marshal Daun.

Washington, with 7,000 Americans, while pursued by 20,000 British and Hessians under Lord Cornwallis, captured a Hessian advance column at Trenton (Dec. 25, 1776) and destroyed a British detachment at Princeton, (Jan. 3, 1777).

Bonaparte, with 30,000 infantry, 3,000 cavalry and 40 cannon, invaded Italy, (March 26, 1796) which was defended by 100,000 Piedmontese and Austrian regulars under Generals Colli and Beaulieu. In fifteen days he had captured the former, driven the latter to his own country and compelled Piedmont to sign a treaty of peace and alliance with France.

At Castiglione, Arcole, Bassano and Rivoli, with an army not exceeding 40,000 men Bonaparte destroyed four Austrian armies, each aggregating about 100,000 men.

At Wagram, Napoleon, with less than 100,000 men, overthrew the main Austrian army of 150,000 men, foiled the attempts at succor of the secondary Austrian army of 40,000 men, and compelled Austria to accept peace with France.

In the campaign of 1814, Napoleon, with never more than 70,000 men, twice repulsed from the walls of Paris and drove backward nearly to the Rhine River an allied army of nearly 300,000 Austrians, Prussians and Russians.

In the year 480 B.C., Xerxes, King of Persia, invaded Greece with an army, which by Herodotus, Plutarch and Isocrates, is estimated at 2,641,610 men at arms and exclusive of servants, butlers, women and camp followers.

Arriving at the Pass of Thermopolae, the march of the invaders was arrested by Leonidas, King of Sparta, with an army made up of 300 Spartans, 400 Thebans, 700 Thespians, 1,000 Phocians and 3,000 from various Grecian States, posted behind a barricade built across the entrance.

This celebrated defile is about a mile in length. It runs between Mount Oeta and an impassible morass, which forms the edge of the Gulf of Malia and at each end is so narrow that a wagon can barely pass.

Xerxes at once sent a herald who demanded of the Grecians the surrender of their arms, to which Leonidas replied:

"Come and take them."

On the fifth day the Persian army attacked, but was unable to force an entrance into the pass. On the sixth day the Persian Immortals likewise were repulsed, and on the seventh day these troops again failed.

That night Ephialtes, a Malian, informed Xerxes of a foot path around the mountains to the westward, and a Persian detachment was sent by a night march en surprise against the Grecian rear. On the approach of this hostile body, the Phocians, who had been detailed by Leonidas to guard this path, abandoned their post without fighting and fled to the summit of the mountains, leaving the way open to the enemy, who, wasting no time in pursuit, at once marched against the rear of the Grecian position.

At the command of Leonidas, all his allies, with the exception of the 700 Thespians, who refused to leave him, abandoned Thermopolae in haste and returned safely to their own countries.

Xerxes waited until day was well advanced and his detachment had taken post upon the Grecian rear. Then both Persian columns attacked simultaneously. The first part of this final conflict was fought outside and to the north of the barricade. Leonidas being slain and their numbers reduced over half, the remaining Greeks retired behind the barricade and took post upon a slight elevation, where one after another they were killed by arrows and javelins. The four days of fighting cost the Persians over 20,000 of their best troops.

Upon the summit of the hill where the Spartans perished a marble lion was erected, bearing the inscription:

"Go tell the Lacedymonians, O, Stranger,

That we died here in obedience to the law."

A second inscription engraved upon a stone column erected upon the scene of conflict read:

"Upon this spot four thousand Pelleponesians contended against three hundred myriads."

The largest army commanded by Epaminondas was about 70,000 men. Alexander the Great, after Arbela, had 135,000 trained troops. Hannibal never led more than 60,000 men in action, nor Caesar more than 80,000. Gustavus Adolphus, just before Lutzen, marshalled 75,000 of the best soldiers in the world under the banners of Protestantism. Turenne never fought with more than 40,000 troops; Prince Eugene often had 150,000 in hand, and Frederic the Great several times commanded 200,000 men. At Yorktown, Washington had 16,000 Continentals, 6,000 French regulars and 18,000 Provincial volunteers; Napoleon's largest army, that of the Austerlitz campaign, consisted of 180,000 men, while von Moltke personally directed at Sadowa, 250,000 men; at Gravelotte, 211,000 men and at Sedan, 200,000 men.

Perfection in Numbers is attained whenever the kindred army has the most troops in the theatre of decisive action.

TIME

"You lose the time for action in frivolous deliberations. Your generals instead of appearing at the head of your armies, parade in processions and add splendor to public ceremonies. Your armies are composed of mercenaries, the dregs of foreign nations, vile robbers, a terror only to yourselves and your allies. Indecision and confusion prevail in your counsels; your projects have neither plan nor foresight. You are the slaves of circumstance and opportunities continually escape you. You hurry aimlessly hither and thither and arrive only in time to witness the success of your enemy."—Demosthenes.

TIME

"That greatest of all advantages—TIME!"—Frederic the Great.

"Ask me for anything except—TIME."—Napoleon.

"Time is the cradle of hope, the grave of ambition, the solitary counsel of the wise and the stern corrector of fools. Wisdom walks before it, opportunities with it and repentance behind it. He that hath made it his friend hath nothing to fear from his enemies, but he that hath made it his enemy hath little to hope even from his friends."—Anon.

———————

The absolute advantage of Time consists in being able to move while the adversary must remain stationary.

The conditioned advantage in Time i.e., the Initiative, consists in artificially restricting the adverse ability to move.

Advantage in Time is divided into two classes:

I. The Initiative.

II. Absolute.

The Initiative treats of restrictions to the movements of an army, due to the necessity of supporting, covering or sustaining Points or corps d'armee, menaced with capture by adverse corps offensive.

The absolute advantage in Time is the ability to move, while the adverse army must remain immovable.

Whenever the right to move is unrestricted, any desired Piece may be moved to any desired Point.

But whenever the right to move is restricted it follows that the Piece desired cannot be moved; or, that if moved it cannot be moved to the desired Point; or, that a piece not desired, must be moved and usually to a Point not desired.

Such restrictions of the right to move, quickly produce fatal defects in the kindred Formation; and from the fact that such fatal defects in Formation can be produced by restricting the right to move, arises the inestimable value of the advantage in Time.

Perfection in Time is attained whenever the kindred army is able to move while the hostile army must remain stationary.

The object of the active or absolute advantage in Time always is to remain with the Initiative, or Passive Advantage in Time; which consists in operating by the movement made, such menaces, as compel the enemy:

1. To move corps d'armee which he otherwise would not move and
2. Prevents him from moving corps d'armee which he otherwise would move.

PRINCIPLE

Given superior brute strength and no matter how blunderingly and clumsily it be directed, it always will end by accomplishing its purpose, unless it is opposed by Skill.

Skill is best manifested by the proper use of Time. Such ability is acquired only through study and experience, guided by reflection, and it can be retained only by systematic and unremitting practice.

Most people imagine that Skill is to be attained merely from study; many believe it but the natural and necessary offshoot of long experience; and there are some of the opinion that dilettante dabbling in book lore is an all-sufficient substitute for that sustained and laborious mental and physical effort, which alone can make perfect in the competitive arts.

Only by employing his leisure in reflection upon the events of the Past can one get to understand those things which make for success in Warfare and in Chessplay, and develop that all-essential ability to detect equivalents in any situation.

For in action there is no time for such reflection, much less for development.

Then, moments of value inestimable for the achieving of results are not to be wasted in the weighing and comparison of things, whose relative importance should be discerned in the twinkling of an eye, by reason of prior familiarity with similar conditions.

The relative advantage in time possessed by one army over an opposing army always can be determined by the following, viz.:

RULE

1. *That army which is in motion while the opposing army must remain stationary has the absolute advantage in Time.*

2. *That army which although at rest can dictate the movement of an opposing army in motion has the conditioned advantage in Time, i.e., the Initiative.*

"One may lose more by letting slip a decisive opportunity than afterwards can be gained by ten battles."—Gustavus Adolphus.

"It is the exact moment that must be seized; one minute too soon or too late and the movement is utterly futile."—Napoleon.

MILITARY EXAMPLES

"The movements of an army should be characterized by decision and rapidity."—Hannibal.

"In order to escape from a dilemma it first of all is necessary to gain Time."—Napoleon.

Thebes having revolted, Alexander the Great marched 400 miles in fourteen days; attacked and captured the city and razed it to the ground (335 B.C.) sparing only the house and family of Pindar, the poet; massacred all males capable of bearing arms and sold 30,000 women and children into slavery.

To gain time to occupy the Strategic center and to cut the communications with Rome of the army of the Consul Flaminius, Hannibal marched his army for three days and nights through the marshes of the Po.

Caesar marched from Rome to Sierra-Modena in Spain, a distance of 1350 miles in twenty-three days.

Frederic the Great in order to gain time usually marched at midnight.

Bonaparte finished his first Italian campaign by winning the battles of St. Michaels, Rivoli and Mantua, marching 200 miles and taking 20,000 prisoners, all in less than four days. In 1805, the French infantry in the manoeuvres which captured 60,000 Austrians, marched from 25 to 30 miles a day. In 1806 the French infantry pursued the Prussians at the same speed. In 1814, Napoleon's army marched at the rate of 30 miles per day, besides fighting a battle every 24 hours. Retrograding for the succor of Paris, Napoleon marched 75 miles in thirty-six hours. On the return from Elba, 1815, the Imperial Guard marched 50 miles the first day, 200 miles in six days and reached Paris, a distance of 600 miles, in twenty days.

"The fate of a battle always is decided by the lack of the few minutes required to bring separated bodies of troops into co- operation."— *Napoleon.*

POSITION

POSITION

"War is a business of position."—Napoleon.

By the term Position is signified those relative advantages and disadvantages in location, which appertain to the aggregate posts occupied by the kindred army, as compared with the aggregate posts occupied by the adverse army.

Advantages and disadvantages in Position are of three classes, viz.:

(a) Those which appertain to the Column of Attack

(b) Those which appertain to the Column of Support.

(c) Those which appertain to the Column of Manoeuvre.

STRATEGETIC SITUATIONS

A Strategic Situation, and whether in warfare or in Chess-play, is produced by the presence, in any Strategetic Plane, *i.e.*, theatre of conflict, of two or more opposing Strategetic Entireties, *i.e.*, contending armies.

These latter are of four classifications and are denominated as follows:

(a) The Kindred Determinate Force.

(b) The Adverse Determinate Force.

(c) The Kindred Hypothetical Force.

(d) The Adverse Hypothetical Force.

RULE I

Given the Strategetic Entireties present in a given Strategetic Situation, designate the opposing Prime Strategetic Factors and express the relative values of each in the terms of the Strategic Syllogism.

THE STRATEGIC SYLLOGISM

Having classified the existing Strategetic Situation, it is necessary next to designate the opposing Columns of Attack, of Support, and of Manoeuvre.

Then, by comparing these Prime Strategetic Factors, to determine the net advantage, disadvantage, or equality that exist between them and to express this condition in the terms of the resulting Strategic Syllogism.

In the construction of a Strategic Syllogism, the Strategic, *i.e.*, the positional value of each of the opposing Prime Strategetic Factors contained in a given Strategetic Situation, is expressed in terms made up of letters and symbols, viz.,

A	Signifies	Column of Attack.
S	"	Column of Support.
M	"	Column of Manoeuvre.
+	"	Advantage in Position.
-	"	Disadvantage in Position.
=	"	Equality in Position.

The positional values of the several Prime Strategetic Factors are obtained as follows:

COLUMN OF ATTACK

That Column of Attack which is posted upon the superior Strategic front as compared to the front occupied by the immediately opposing formation (cf, Grand Tactics, pp. 117 to 275), has the advantage in position.

This relative advantage and disadvantage in position of the Column of Attack is expressed by the first term of the Strategic Syllogism, viz.:

(I.)

$$\frac{+A}{-A}$$

or

(II.)

$$\frac{-A}{+A}$$

In the first instance (I), the White Column of Attack has the advantage and the Black formation has the disadvantage; in the second case (II), this condition is reversed.

A Column of Support has the superiority in position, as compared with the adverse Column of Support, whenever it contains more than the latter of the following advantages, viz.:

I. One, or more, Passed Pawns.

II. Two united Pawns, overlapping an adverse Pawn.

III. Two isolated Pawns adjacent to a single adverse Pawn.

IV. Three, or more, united Pawns at their fifth squares, opposed by a like number of adverse Pawns posted on their Normal Base Line.

V. A majority of kindred Pawns on that side of the Board farthest from the adverse King.

The relative advantage and disadvantage of one Column of Support, over the opposing Column of Support, is expressed by the second term of the Strategic Syllogism, thus:

(I.)

$$\frac{+S}{-S}$$

or

(II.)

$$\frac{-S}{+S}$$

In the first case (I), White has the advantage and Black has the disadvantage. In the second case (II), this condition is reversed.

Columns of Manoeuvre are not compared with each other. The advantage of one over another is determined by comparing their respective powers of

113

resistance to the attack of the corresponding adverse Columns of Support.

That Column of Manoeuvre which longest can debar the adverse promotable Factors from occupying a point of junction on the kindred Strategetic Rear, has the advantage.

The relative advantage and disadvantage of the column of Manoeuvre is expressed by the third term of the Strategic Syllogism, viz.:

(I.)

$$\frac{+M}{-M}$$

or

(II.)

$$\frac{-M}{+M}$$

In the first case (I), White, has the advantage and Black the disadvantage. In the second case (II), this condition is reversed.

In recording the values of the opposing Prime Strategetic Factors, the terms relating to White are written above and those relating to Black, below the line.

The terms expressing the relative values of the Columns of Attack always are placed at the left; those for the Columns of Support in the center, and those for the Columns of Manoeuvre at the right.

The Strategic Syllogisms are twenty-seven in number and are formulated, viz.:

TABLE OF STRATEGIC SYLLOGISMS

No. 1. $\dfrac{+A+S+M}{-A-S-M}$

No. 2. $\dfrac{+A+S=M}{-A-S=M}$

No. 3. $\dfrac{+A+S-M}{-A-S+M}$

No. 4.
$$\frac{+A=S+M}{-A=S-M}$$

No. 5.
$$\frac{+A=S=M}{-A=S=M}$$

No. 6.
$$\frac{+A=S-M}{-A=S+M}$$

No. 7.
$$\frac{+A-S+M}{-A+S-M}$$

No. 8.
$$\frac{+A-S=M}{-A+S=M}$$

No. 9.
$$\frac{+A-S-M}{-A+S+M}$$

No. 10.
$$\frac{=A+S+M}{=A-S-M}$$

No. 11.
$$\frac{=A+S=M}{=A-S=M}$$

No. 12.
$$\frac{=A+S-M}{=A-S+M}$$

No. 13.
$$\frac{=A=S+M}{=A=S-M}$$

No. 14.
$$\frac{=A=S=M}{=A=S=M}$$

No. 15.
$$\frac{=A=S-M}{=A=S+M}$$

No. 16.
$$\frac{=A-S+M}{=A+S-M}$$

No. 17.
$$\frac{=A-S=M}{=A+S=M}$$

No. 18.
$$\frac{=A-S-M}{=A+S+M}$$

No. 19. $\dfrac{-A+S+M}{+A-S-M}$

No. 20. $\dfrac{-A+S=M}{+A-S=M}$

No. 21. $\dfrac{-A+S-M}{+A-S+M}$

No. 22. $\dfrac{-A=S+M}{+A=S-M}$

No. 23. $\dfrac{-A=S=M}{+A=S=M}$

No. 24. $\dfrac{-A=S-M}{+A=S+M}$

No. 25. $\dfrac{-A-S+M}{+A+S-M}$

No. 26. $\dfrac{-A-S=M}{+A+S=M}$

No. 27. $\dfrac{-A-S-M}{+A+S+M}$

STRATEGIC ELEMENTALS.

Each of the terms contained in the Strategic Syllogism should have its counterpart in a tangible and competent mass of troops.

This principle of Strategetics, when applied to warfare, is absolute, and admits of no exception. The catastrophies sustained by the French armies in the campaigns of 1812, 1813, 1814 and 1815 are each and every one directly due to the persistent violation by Napoleon of this basic truth, in devolving the duties of a column of support and a column of manoeuvre upon a single Strategic Elemental.

In solemn contrast to that fatal and indefensible rashness which cost Napoleon five great armies and ultimately his crown, is the dictum by one whose transcendent success in warfare, is the antithesis of the utter ruination which terminated the career of the famous Corsican.

Says Frederic the Great:

*"I adhere to those universal laws which all the elements obey;
these, for me are sufficient."*

Singularly enough, it seemingly has escaped the notice of the great in warfare, owing to the subtle mathematical construction of the Chess-board, its peculiar relations to the moves of the Chess-pieces, and of the latter to each other, that:

PRINCIPLE

I. The functions of all three terms contained in a Strategic Syllogism may be combined in a single chess Pawn, and, that:

II. All three functions are contemplated in and should be expressed by every movement of every Chess-piece; and every move upon the Chess-board is weak and unscientific, to the extent that it disregards either of these obligations.

Those advantages in position, which are denoted by the plus signs of the Strategic Syllogism, have their material manifestation upon the surface of the earth by Corps d'armee, and by Pieces which are equivalents of these latter, upon the Chess-board.

The *sign +A in the Strategic Syllogism* denotes the superior Strategic Front. That point whose occupation by a kindred piece demonstrates such superiority in position is termed the *Key of Position*. The kindred Corps occupying such point constitutes a *Corps en Line*, and is termed the *First Strategic Elemental*.

The *sign +S in the Strategic Syllogism* denotes the *larger number* of pawn altitudes open to the kindred promotable factors. Those points occupied by such kindred promotable factors are termed *Logistic Origins*. The kindred Corps which occupy such points constitute *Corps en Route* and collectively are termed the *Second Strategic Elemental*. The objective of Corps en Route always is the Kindred Logistic Horizon.

The *sign +M in the Strategic Syllogism* denotes that the *shortest* open pawn altitude is occupied by a kindred promotable factor. Such kindred promotable factor is termed the *Corps en Touch*, and the point occupied by such Corps is termed the *Point of Proximity*. The Objective of such Corps always is a designated Point of Junction in the Kindred Logistic Horizon, and such Corps constitutes the *Third Strategic Elemental*.

In Warfare it is imperative that each of these Strategic Elementals be represented by one or more Corps d'armee. But it is a second peculiarity of the Chessic mechanism that a single Chessic Corps d'armee may represent in itself, one, two or three Strategic Elementals and thus constitute even the entire *Strategic Ensemble.*

Hence, in Chess play, the Strategic Ensemble may be either single, double, or triple, viz.:

A Single Strategic Ensemble consists either of:

(a) 1. Major Vertex.

2. Grand Vertex.

(b) Logistic Origin.

(c) Point of Proximity.

A *Double Strategic Ensemble* consists of either:

(a) 1. Major Vertex, plus a Kindred Logistic Origin.

2. Grand Vertex, plus a Kindred Logistic Origin.

(b) 1. Major Vertex, plus a Kindred Point of Proximity.

2. Grand Vertex, plus a Kindred Point of Proximity.

(c) Logistic Origin, plus a Kindred Point of Proximity.

A *Triple Strategic Ensemble* consists of:

1. Major Vertex, plus a Kindred Logistic Origin, plus a Kindred Point of Proximity.

2. Grand Vertex, plus a Kindred Point of Proximity, plus a Kindred Logistic Origin.

PRINCIPLE

The relative positional advantage expressed by the plus signs of the Strategic Syllogism decreases as the number of plus signs in the Strategic Syllogism exceeds the number of corresponding Strategic Elementals.

Failure to observe the amalgamation of the duties of the three Grand Columns in each and every move upon the Chess-board, and to note that the tangible and material expression of these powers and advantages may be expressed either by three, by two, or even by a single Chessic Corps d'armee, has caused doubt of the exact analogy between Chess and War; and hence a like doubt of the utility of Chess-play.

Recognizing the truth of the foregoing, the Asiatic conqueror, Tamerlane, sought to rectify this discrepancy between the mechanism of Chess and that of War, by increasing the size of the Chess-board to one hundred and forty- four squares, and the number of pieces to forty-eight.

By this innovation the geometric harmony existing between the Dynamic and the Static surfaces of the Chess-board was destroyed; and this without substituting therefor another like condition of mathematic perfection. Ultimately, this remedy was abandoned, a fate which sooner or later, has overtaken all attempts to improve that superlative intellectual exercise of which says Voltaire:

"Of all games, Chess does most honor to the human mind."

The reason why the scheme devised by Tamerlane did not satisfy even himself, and why all attempted alterations in the machinery of Chess prove unacceptable in practice, is due to the present perfect adaptation of the Board and the Pieces for exemplifying the processes of Strategetic Art.

Any change in the construction of the Chess-board and the Chess-pieces, to be effective, must largely increase the number of Chessmen, correspondingly increase the number of squares, and equally so, increase the number of moves permitted to each player at his turn to play.

That is to say: Such innovation to be correct must permit each player at his turn to play to move one of the Corps d'armee contained in the Column of Attack, a second in the Column of Support, and a third in the Column of Manoeuvre. Necessarily, the number of pieces must be increased in order to provide Corps d'armee for the make-up of each Grand Column, and obviously, the Board must be sufficiently enlarged to accommodate not merely this increased mass, but also to permit full scope for the increased number of possible movements.

The student thus readily will perceive, that it is only one step from such an elaboration of Chess, to an army and the theatre of actual campaigning.

Perfection in Position is attained whenever the kindred army is acting or is posted as a unit, while the hostile army is not so posted nor able so to act.

MILITARY EXAMPLES

COLUMN OF ATTACK

"Frontal attacks are to be avoided, and the preference always is to be given to the assault of a single wing, with your center and remaining wing held back; because if your attack is successful you equally destroy the enemy without the risk of being routed if you fail."—Frederic the Great.

At Leuctra and Mantinea, Epaminondas won by the oblique or Strategic order of battle. Alexander the Great won by the same order at Issus and the Haspades. Cyrus won at Thymbra and Hannibal won at Trebia, Thrasymene, Cannae and Herdonea, by the three sides of an octagon or enveloping formation. Caesar won by the oblique order at Pharsaleus.

Gustavus Adolphus won at Leipsic by acting from the Tactical Center and Turenne and Prince Eugene gained their victories by the same means.

Frederic the Great won at Hohenfriedberg, Sohr, Rosbach, Leuthern, Zorndorf and Leignitz by the oblique order and at Torgau by acting from the tactical center.

Washington won at Trenton and Princeton acting by three contiguous sides of an octagon.

Bonaparte won at Montenotte, Castiglione, Arcola, Rivoli, Ulm, Austerlitz, Jena, Friedland, Wagram and Ligny, by acting from the tactical center. Never did he attack by the oblique order of battle.

Von Moltke's victories all were won by acting in strict accord with the system laid down for the use of the Prussian army by Frederic the Great.

COLUMN OF SUPPORT

The most magnificent illustration both of the proper and of the improper use of the Column of Support is found in that Grand Operation executed by the Roman consuls, Claudius Nero and Marcus Livius, whereby the Carthagenian Army under Hasdrubal was destroyed at the river Metaurus 207 B.C.

Hannibal, with the main Carthagenian army, posted in the south of Italy near Canusium, was observed by Nero and his troops; while in the west, Hasdrubal, observed by Livius was slowly advancing southward to form a junction with his brother, a most unscientific procedure.

Livius permitted Hasdrubal to penetrate into Italy to a point a few miles south of the Metaurus River; whereupon Nero, taking 7,000 of his best troops, by a rapid march of 200 miles united with Livius; and the two consuls at once falling upon Hasdrubal utterly annihilated the Carthagenian army. Nero returned at all speed and the first news of his march and of the death blow to the Carthagenian projects against Rome was furnished by the sight of his brother's head, which Nero cast into Hannibal's camp from a military machine.

The true method for uniting the Columns of Support to a Column of Attack is thus shown by Gustavus Adolphus:

"We encamped about Nuremberg the middle of June, the army after so many detachments was not above 11,000 infantry and 8,000 horse and dragoons. The King posted his army in the suburbs and drew intrenchments around the circumference so that he begirt the whole city with his army. His works were large, the ditch deep, planked by innumerable bastions, ravelins, horn-works, forts, redoubts, batteries and palisades, the incessant labor of 8000 men for fourteen days.

"On the 30th of June the Imperialists, joined to the Bavarian army arrived and sat down 60,000 strong, between the city and the friendly states; in order to intercept the King's provisions and to starve him out.

"The King had three great detachments and several smaller ones, acting abroad, reducing to his power the castles and towns of the adjacent countries and these he did not hasten to join him until their work was done.

"The two chief armies had now lain for five or six weeks in sight of each other and the King thinking all was ready, ordered his generals to join him. Gustavus Horn was on the Moselle, Chancellor Oxenstern about Mentz and Cologne and Dukes William and Bernard and Gen. Bannia in Bavaria.

"Our friends were not backward in obeying the King's command, and having drawn together their forces from various parts and *ALL* joined the chancellor Oxenstern, they set out in full march for Nuremburg, where they arrived Aug. 21, being 30,000 old soldiers commanded by officers of the greatest conduct and experience in the world."

Only once, at the battle of Torgau, (Nov. 5, 1760) did Frederick the Great rely upon the co-operation of his Columns of Support for victory.

As the result, his Column of Attack of 25,000 men fought the entire battle and was so ruined by the fire and sabres of 90,000 enemies and 400 pieces of artillery that, as the sun went down the King charged at the head of two battalions, his sole remaining troops. At this moment Gen. Zeithen, with the Column of Support, of 22,000 men occupied Siptka Hill, the tactical key of the battlefield, and fired a salvo of artillery to inform the King of their presence. The astonished Austrians turned and fled; the King's charge broke their line of battle and Frederic grasped a victory, "for which" says Napoleon, "he was indebted to Fortune and the only one in which he displayed no talent."

This comment of course is not true. Frederic displayed magnificent talent that day, by holding in check a force of thrice his numbers and so shattering it by his incessant attacks that it crumbled to pieces before the mere presence and at sight of his fresh and vigorous Column of Support. Had Napoleon displayed such talent in the personal conduct of battles during 1813, 1814 and 1815 it is possible that he would have terminated his career at some other place than at St. Helena.

The experience, however, was enough to fully satisfy Frederic, and never again did he attempt a Logistic battle.

The capture of Lord Cornwallis at Yorktown is perhaps the nearest approach to the achievement of Nero and Livius in the annals of the military art. Decoyed by the retrograde movements of Gen. Greene, the British army was deluded into taking up a position at Yorktown, having the unfordable

James River in rear, and within striking distance of the main American army under Washington about New York City.

Lafayette was ordered to reinforce Greene; Count d'Esting was induced to bring the French fleet from the West Indies to Chesapeake Bay to prevent the rescue of Cornwallis by British coming by the ocean, and Count Rochambeau was requested to join Washington with the French army then in Rhode Island.

All this took time, but everything was executed like clockwork. The French fleet arrived in the Chesapeake; the next day came a British fleet to rescue the Earl's army. In the naval fight which ensued, the British were driven to sea and so damaged as to compel their return to New York. By a swift march, Washington, with his Continentals and the French, joined Greene and Lafayette, and two of his redoubts being taken by storm, Lord Cornwallis surrendered. This victory established the independence of the American Colonies.

———————

The Logistic Battle, *i.e.*, the combination of the Columns of Attack and of Support was first favorite with Napoleon and to his partiality for this particular form of the tactical offensive was due both the spectacular successes and the annihilating catastrophes which mark his astonishing career.

The retrieving of his lost battle of Marengo, by the fortuitous arrival of Dessaix column, seems to have impressed Napoleon to the extent that he ever after preferred to win by such process, rather than by any other.

The first attempt to put his new hypothesis into practice was at Jena. Single handed his column of attack destroyed the Prussian main body, while Davoust with the column of manoeuvre held in check over three times his numbers.

The French Column of Support under Bernadotte did not arrive in season to fire a shot.

———————

At Eylau, the French Column of Support under Davoust was four hours in advancing six miles against the opposition of the Russian general Doctoroff. The second French Column of Support under Ney did not reach the field until the battle was over.

———————

In the retreat from Russia, the French Column of Support under the Duke of Belluno was driven from its position at Smolensko, thus permitting the Russians under Kutosof to occupy the Strategic center, which disaster cost Napoleon 30,000 men in clearing his communications.

In 1813, the Column of Support under Ney at Bautzen was misdirected and the battle rendered indecisive by its lack of co-operation with the French Column of Attack.

In 1814, Napoleon conformed to the Art by acting in three columns, but yielding to his besetting military sin, he joined his Column of Support to his Column of Attack and through the open space thus created in the French Strategetic Front, Blucher advanced triumphantly to Paris.

In the Waterloo campaign, Napoleon properly began with three Grand Columns. At the battle of Ligny, his Column of Support arrived upon Blucher's left flank and then without firing a shot, wheeled about and marched away.

At Waterloo, by uniting his Columns of Attack and of Support prematurely, Napoleon permitted Blucher to penetrate the French Strategetic Front and to win in the same manner and as decisively as he did at Paris.

Von Moltke won the battle of Sadowa by the arrival of the Prussian Column of Support, commanded by Prince Frederic William. But in the interim, the German main army was driven in several miles by the Austrians, and Prince Bismark's first white hairs date from that day.

COLUMN OF MANOEUVRE

"A small body of brave and expert men, skillfully handled and

favored by the ground, easily may render difficult the advance of a large army."—Frederic the Great.

At the river Metaurus, the Roman Consul Livius gave a fine example of the duties of a Column of Manoeuvre which are slowly and securely to retreat before an advancing enemy and never to be induced into a pitched battle until the arrival of the kindred main body.

Frederic the Great made great use of Columns of Manoeuvre. In the Seven Years War he constantly maintained such a column against the armies of each State with whom Prussia was at war; while himself and his brother Henry operated as Columns of Attack.

In the Revolutionary War, Washington maintained a Column of Manoeuvre against the British in Rhode Island, another against the British in the south and a third against the hostile Indian tribes of the southwest.

Napoleon constantly used Columns of Manoeuvre in all his campaigns; notably at Montenotte, Castiglione, Arcole, Rivoli, Ulm, Austerlitz, Jena, in 1812, 1813, 1814 and at Ligny and Waterloo in 1815.

PRIME STRATEGETIC MEANS

PRIME STRATEGETIC MEANS

"It is necessary exactly to weigh the means we possess in opposition to the enemy in order to determine beforehand which must ultimately predominated."—Frederic the Great.

———————

Those elemental quantities whose comparative values are determined by Grand Reconnaissance and which are termed: Organization, Topography, Mobility, Numbers, Time, and Position, collectively constitute Prime Strategetic Means whose proper employment is the basis of every true Prime Strategetic Process.

POLICY OF CAMPAIGN

That relative advantage in Numbers expressed by the larger aggregate of Chess-pieces is materially manifested upon the Chess-board by additional geometric and sub-geometric symbols.

Excess or deficiency in Numbers determines the policy of Campaign. The policy of the inferior force is:

1. To preserve intact its Corps d'armee, and

2. To engage in battle only when victory can be assured by other advantages in Strategetic means, which nullify the adverse advantage in Numbers; and even then only when such victory is decisive of the Campaign.

Hence, the policy of Campaign of that army superior in Numbers, is:

Incessantly to proffer battles which:

(a) Accepted, constantly reduces the inferior army and increases its disproportion in numbers, or,

(b) Evaded, compels the inferior army to abandon important posts, for whose defence it cannot afford the resulting loss of troops; thus permitting to the numerically superior army a continually increasing advantage in Position.

PRINCIPLE

All else being equal the advantage of Numbers is decisive of victory in battle and Campaign.

Things being unequal, the advantage in Numbers may be nullified by adverse advantages in Organization, Topography, Mobility, Time and Position.

Victory resulting from advantage in Numbers is achieved by simultaneously attacking two or more Tactical Keys from a Kindred Strategic Key and two or more Kindred Points of Command.

TO LOCATE THE AREA OF CONCENTRATION

That *relative advantage in Mobility* expressed by the situation of the Strategic Front upon the Strategetic Center is materially manifested upon the Chess-board by Kindred Chess-pieces posted upon that great central diagonal which extends towards the Objective Plane. Such advantage determines those points which should be occupied in the proper development of the front so posted; and consequently designates the direction and location of that battlefield upon which the kindred army may concentrate in overwhelming force, despite all possible resistance by the enemy.

MOST FAVORABLE BATTLEFIELD

That *relative advantage in Organization* expressed by superior potential totality, is materially manifested upon the Chess-board by the geometric and sub-geometric symbols of those Chess-pieces possessed of the superior potential complement. Such symbols taken in combination, describe that field of battle most favorable for the execution of those Major Tactical evolutions which appertain to the Chess-pieces of superior organization.

POSTS OF MAXIMUM SECURITY

That *relative defensive advantage in Topography* expressed by inaccessibility to hostile attack is materially manifested upon the Chess-board by Corps of Position, posted upon points of different color to that occupied by the adverse Bishop; and this advantage designates those posts situated on a projected field of battle which may be occupied with the maximum of security.

That *relative offensive advantage in Topography* expressed by accessibility to kindred attack is materially manifested upon the Chess-board by Corps of Position posted upon points of the same color as that occupied by the kindred Bishop; and this advantage designates those posts situated on a projected field of battle which may be attacked with the maximum facility.

CHARACTER OF THE MOST FAVORABLE BATTLE

That *relative advantage in Position with the Column of Attack*, expressed:

1. By superior location, direction and development of the Kindred Strategic Front of Operations; and

2. By the occupation of Points of Departure, of Manoeuvre, of Command and of the Strategic Key of a True Strategic Horizon, indicates that a Strategic Grand Battle in the first instance; and in the second case that a Tactical Grand Battle is most favorable in the existing situation.

That *relative advantage in Position with the Column of Support*, expressed by superior facilities for occupying with the Kindred Promotable Factors their corresponding Points of Junction in the Kindred Logistic Horizon, is materially manifested upon the Chess-board by the larger number of Pawn Altitudes which either are open, or may be opened, despite all possible resistance by the enemy; and such advantage designates those adverse Points of Impenetrability and Points of Resistance to the march of the Kindred Promotable Factors, which it is necessary to nullify.

That *relative advantage in Position with the Column of Manoeuvre*, expressed by the security of the Kindred and the exposure of the adverse Strategetic Rear to attack by the Kindred Column of Support, is materially manifested upon the Chess-board by the occupation by a Kindred Promotable Factor of the Point of Proximity; and such advantage indicates that the advance with all possible celerity of such Promotable Factor and Point of Proximity toward the corresponding Point of Junction is a dominating influence in the existing situation.

PROJECTED GRAND BATTLE

From the advantage in Position appertaining to the three Grand Columns is deduced the character of the Grand Battle properly in sequence.

Advantage in Position with the Column of Attack indicates the opportunity, all else being equal, to engage in a victorious Strategic Grand Battle against the hostile Formation in Mass, or in a Tactical Grand Battle against the hostile Formation by Wings.

Advantage in Position with the Column of Support indicates the opportunity to engage effectively in a series of minor battles, as though having the advantage in Numbers.

Advantage in Position with the Column of Manoeuvre indicates the opportunity to engage in a victorious Logistic Grand Battle against the adverse Formation by Grand Columns.

LEAST FAVORABLE ADVERSE CONDITION

That *relative advantage in Time* expressed by restrictions of the adversary's choice of movements at his turn to play, is materially manifested upon the Chess-board by Feints operated by Kindred Chess-pieces against adverse vital points; and such advantage of the Initiative dictates the next move of the opposing army.

The *advantage of the Initiative* determines which of the adverse corps d'armee may and may not move.

The material expression of this advantage always is a Feint by a Kindred Corps against a vital point either occupied or unoccupied, which necessitates that upon his next move, the enemy either evacuate, support, cover or sustain the post so menaced.

Such feint, therefore, restricts the move of the enemy to those of his corps as are able to obviate the threatened loss and proportionately reduces the immediate activity of his army.

RELATIVE ADVANTAGES IN LOCATION

"It is only the force brought into action that avails in battles and campaigns—the rest does not count."—Napoleon.

The distance which separates opposing Corps d'armee always modifies the values of the Prime Strategetic Means.

Hence in the making of Grand Reconnaissance, it is next in sequence to determine whether the Chess-pieces are:

I. In Contact.

II. In Presence.

III. At Distance.

Corps d'armee are *in Contact* with each other whenever their logistic radii intersect; or, their radii offensive and the corresponding adverse radii defensive are opposed to each other.

Corps d'armee are *in Presence* whenever the posts which they occupy are contained within the same Strategic front, the same Strategetic Horizon, or are in communication with their corresponding posts of mobilization, development, or manoeuvre.

Corps d'armee are *at Distance* when the posts which they occupy are not in communication with Kindred Corps d'armee posted upon the strategic front adopted, or with posts of mobilization or development contained within the corresponding Primary Base of Operations, or, within the True Strategetic Horizon.

REQUISITES FOR SUCCESSFUL CAMPAIGNING

Every Campaign, whether upon the surface of the Earth or upon the Chess-board is decided and usually is terminated by a Grand Battle.

Those movements of opposing Grand Columns, whereby such decisive conflict is brought about under circumstances which ensure victory, by reason of superior advantages in Strategetic Means, are termed Grand Manoeuvres; and a proper series of Grand Manoeuvres, combined with their corresponding feints, strategems, ambuscades and minor battles, the whole terminated by a resulting Grand Battle, is termed a Grand Operation.

Those processes of Grand Manoeuvre, which produce an opportunity to victoriously engage in battle, are the most subtle and difficult known to the Strategetic Art.

Successful application of these processes in practice depends wholly upon proper use of the MEANS at hand and the doing of the utmost that can be done in the TIME available.

Nothing can be more repugnant to high art in Strategetics than those crudities termed in the specious mouthings of pretentious mediocrity "waiting moves," "delayed strokes," "defensive-offensives," "masterly inactivities," and the like.

"Time past is gone and cannot be regained; time future is not and may never be; time present is" and with it Opportunity, which an instant later may be gone.

The gain of but "a foot of ground and a minute of time" would have saved the French army at Rosbach and have cost Frederic the Great one of his most lustrous victories and perhaps his army and his crown.

PRINCIPLE

In Strategetics there is but a single method whereby Opportunity may be availed of, and that is by so augmenting kindred advantages and so depreciating adverse advantages as to acquire for the kindred army that particular advantage of Strategetic means which in the given situation is the proper basis of the Strategetic movement next in sequence.

At Distance.

The chief requisite for success when acting against an adverse army at Distance, is the advantage in MOBILITY.

The primary process is that of a Grand Manoeuvre against an adverse army acting in the formation by Grand Columns, and the object of such Grand Manoeuvre always is, by superior celerity of movement, to occupy:

1. The Strategic Center by the Kindred Column of Attack, thus intersecting the Route of Communication between the adverse main body and its Base of Operation; or to occupy:

2. The Logistic Center with the Kindred Columns of Support and of Manoeuvre, thus intersecting the Route of Communication between the adverse main body and its Chief Supporting Column and clearing the way for the advance of the Kindred Column of Support against the flank and rear of the adverse Main Body.

Obviously, the united Kindred Columns of Attack and of Support always will constitute an overwhelming superiority in Numbers as compared with the adverse main body.

In Presence.

The chief requisite for success when acting against an adverse Grand Column in Presence, is the advantage in POSITION.

The primary process is that of a Grand Manoeuvre against an adverse army acting in the Formation by Wings, and the object of such Grand Manoeuvre always is, by availing to the uttermost of its situation upon the Tactical Center, *i.e.*, upon the area midway between the adverse Wings thus isolated from each other; to act in overwhelming Numbers, first against one and then against the other hostile bodies.

In Contact.

The chief requisite for success when acting offensively against an adverse Grand Column, or Wing, or Corps d'armee, in Contact, is the advantage in NUMBERS.

The primary process is that of a Grand Battle in which the kindred army has an overwhelming superiority in Numbers in contact, and at least the equality in all other Prime Strategetic Means.

In this circumstance, the object of such Grand Battle always is:

1. To attack the hostile Formation in Mass frontally at the center, and upon both wings obliquely; all three attacks being made simultaneously and the evolutions so executed that the hostile army never is able to penetrate between either kindred wing and the kindred center, nor to outflank that kindred wing which may be in the air.

2. In case the kindred army has the equality or inferiority in all other Prime Strategetic Means, then the object of a Grand Battle on the Offensive is to attack the hostile Formation in Mass obliquely with the whole kindred army, and preferably upon that wing which covers the route of communication of the adverse army with its Base of Operations, but always upon that wing which contains the Tactical Key of the actual Battlefield.

Obviously, the concentration of the entire kindred army against a single adverse wing always will constitute an overwhelming superiority in Numbers.

In making such attack obliquely against a single adverse wing, the center and remaining wing of the kindred army must not engage until the kindred Van and Corps of Position of the attacking wing first have formed the *center* of three sides of an octagon; of which the Kindred Corps of Evolution will form the *farthest* side and the Kindred Center and left wing Corps d'armee will form the *nearest* and latest constructed side.

The chief requisite for success when acting defensively against a Grand Column, or Wing, or Corps d'armee is the advantage in TOPOGRAPHY.

The primary process is that of a Grand Battle in which the kindred army, decidedly inferior in Numbers in the aggregate, has the advantage in Topography and equality in all other Prime Strategetic Means.

In this case the object is to support both flanks of the inferior army upon impassable natural barriers, strengthening both wings at the expense of the center, both in quantity and in quality of troops.

If the Tactical Defensive be selected, the center should retire before the oncoming of the hostile army in order to enclose it between the Kindred Wings, which will then overwhelm it by superior Numbers, while the natural barriers on the flanks being impassable will prevent the remaining hostile corps from participating in the battle otherwise than as spectators.

Should the Tactical Offensive be selected, that kindred wing best adapted for attack should engage supported by all kindred Corps of Evolution, while advancing the Kindred Center in reserve and holding the remaining wing refused and in observation.

All else being equal, relative advantage in either branch of Prime Strategetic Means is sufficient to ensure victory in battle, and the proper use of such advantage for securing victory is outlined thus:

PRINCIPLE

Utilize advantage in Prime Strategetic Means to obtain the superiority in Numbers at the Point of Contact in an Offensive Battle; and to nullify the adverse superiority in Numbers at the point of contact in a Defensive Battle.

Between War and Chess there is a seeming incongruity, which is the basis of that doubt of the utility of Chess-play, so commonly held by laymen, and which fallacy few, even among proficients, are competent to combat.

This doubt most frequently is voiced by the query:

If Chess and War are analagous, why was not Napoleon a Master Chess-player and Morphy a great military Commander?

This query readily is answered in the words of Frederic the Great, viz.:

"To be possessed of talent is not sufficient. Opportunity to display such talent and to its full extent is necessary. All depends on the time in which we live."

The Strategetic talent possessed in common by Morphy and Napoleon, in both was brought to perfection by long and expert training.

But circumstances placed the twelve year old Napoleon in the midst of soldiers and in an era of war, while circumstances placed the twelve year old Morphy in the midst of Chess-players and in an era of Peace.

Napoleon was educated a General; Morphy was educated a lawyer.

To develop his self-evident and superlative Strategetic talent, Napoleon's education was of the best; to develop his self-evident and superlative Strategetic talent, Morphy's education was of the worst.

Napoleon succeeded as a General; Morphy failed as a lawyer.

The innate capability of Napoleon for Strategetics was developed in the direction of Warfare; the innate capability of Morphy for Strategetics was developed in the direction of Chess-play.

In War, Napoleon is superlative; in Chess, Morphy is superlative.

Educated in the law, Napoleon might have proved like Morphy a non- entity; educated in Chess, Napoleon might have proved like Morphy a phenomenon.

Educated in War, Morphy might have rivalled Napoleon.

For the Chess-play of Morphy displays that perfect comprehension of Strategetics, to which none but the great Captains in warfare have attained.

Perfection in Strategetics consists in exactly interpreting in battle and campaign, the System of Warfare invented by Epaminondas.

Those able to do this in War have achieved greatness, and the great at Chess-play are those who best have imitated that exactness with which Morphy employed this system on the Chess-board.

To those who imagine that Strategetic talent, as exemplified in Warfare, is different from Strategetic talent as exemplified in Chess-play, the following may afford matter for reflection.

"Frederic the Great was one of the finest Chess-players that Germany ever produced."—Wilhelm Steinitz.

PRIME STRATEGETIC PROPOSITION
SECTION ONE

PRIME STRATEGETIC PROPOSITION
SECTION ONE

(FIRST PHASE.)

In the consideration of every Strategetic Situation possible in Warfare, or in Chess-play, the initial process always is a Grand Reconnaissance.

Grand Reconnaissance is that exact scrutiny of existing conditions, whereby is determined the relative advantages and disadvantages possessed by the opposing armies in:

1. Time.

2. Numbers.

3. Position.

4. Organization.

5. Mobility.

6. Topography.

The *First Phase* in the demonstration of every Prime Strategetic Proposition consists:

1. *In determining by comparison of the relative advantages and disadvantages in Time, which of the opposing armies has the ability to MOVE, while the other must remain stationary.*

2. *In deducing the MOTIF of such movement.*

3. *In designating the DIRECTION of such movement.*

The making of Grand Reconnaissance is a special privilege which exclusively appertains to the advantage in *Time*. It always should be made by the Commander-in-chief of that army which is able to put itself in motion, while the opposing army must remain stationary, and it never should be confounded with the advance of the Cavalry Corps, nor confused with the work of scouts and spies; all of which are matters entirely separate and distinct from Grand Reconnaissance.

In the Grand Reconnaissance of any given Strategetic Situation the element of Numbers *primarily* is to be considered, for the reason that the basic fact of the Science of Strategetics is:

"THE GREATER FORCE ALWAYS OVERCOMES THE LESSER."—Napoleon.

Hence, unless more immediately vital considerations prevent, superiority in Numbers, of itself, is *decisive* of victory; and thus it readily is to be deduced that all else being equal, the advantage in Time plus the advantage in Numbers constitutes the easiest and simplest winning combination known to Strategetic Art.

But it so happens that the advantage in Time may be combined not only with the greater force, but also with an equal, or even with the lesser force, and from this it is self-evident that Strategetic Situations are divided into three classes, viz.:

I. Numerical superiority, plus right to move.

II. Numerical equality, plus right to move.

III. Numerical inferiority, plus right to move.

There are *two primary methods* for availing of superiority in Numbers to destroy the opposing lesser force, viz.:

1. *By the Process of Attrition, i.e., by maintaining an incessant tactical offensive and thus wearing down the opposing army by exchanging pieces at every opportunity.*

2. *By Acting in Detachments, i.e., by means of the extra corps, simultaneously to attack more points of vital importance than the hostile army is able simultaneously to defend.*

From the foregoing it is obvious that conversely there are two principal considerations, which all else being equal, must dominate the procedure of the Numerically inferior force, viz.:

I. To avoid further diminution of its aggregate.

II. To avoid creating indefensible vital points.

———

The *second consideration* in the making of a Grand Reconnaissance by the commander-in-chief of an army having the advantage in Time, is the element of *Position*; for the reason that by unscientific posting of Corps d'armee, relative advantages in Time, or in Numbers or in both, may be rendered nugatory, on account of inability of the kindred Columns of Attack, of Support and of Manoeuvre to perform their functions.

In case the Corps are scientifically posted and are in positions to avail of advantage in Time and Numbers, those adverse vital points whose occupation may be effected by superior force, always will be the objectives of the movements of the latter.

Hence, the following:

PRINCIPLE

As the advantage in Time gives the right to MOVE and the advantage in Numbers indicates the MOTIF of movement; so does the advantage in Position, as expressed by the Strategic Syllogism, specify the DIRECTION of that movement which normally appertains to the army having the advantage in Time.

The proper *direction* of that movement which normally appertains to the advantage in Time always is indicated by the plus signs in the Strategic Syllogism, viz.:

+A. Signifies that the Normal direction of movement for the army having the advantage in Time is along the Strategetic Center towards the Objective Plane.

+S. Signifies that the Normal direction of movement for the army having the advantage in Time is along one or more pawn altitudes towards the Kindred Logistic Horizon.

+M. Signifies that the Normal direction of movement for the army having the advantage in Time is along the shortest open pawn altitude towards the Kindred Point of Junction.

+A+S. Signifies that the Normal direction of movement for the army having the advantage in Time is double, *i.e.*,

+A. towards the Objective Plane.

+S. along one or more open Pawn altitudes toward the Kindred Logistic Horizon.

+A+M. Signifies that the Normal direction of movement for the army having the advantage in Time, is double, *i.e.*,

+A. towards the Objective Plane.

+M. Along the shortest open pawn altitude toward the Kindred

Point of Junction.

_____

+S+M. Signifies that the Normal direction of movement for the army
having the advantage in Time is double, *i.e.*,

+S. Along one or more open Pawn altitudes toward the
Kindred Logistic Horizon.

+M. Along the shortest open Pawn Altitude toward the Kindred
Point of Junction.

_____

+A+S+M. Signifies that the Normal direction of movement is triple, *i.e.*,

+A. Toward the Objective Plane.

+S. Along one or more open Pawn altitudes, toward the
Kindred Logistic Horizon.

+M. Along the shortest open Pawn altitude, toward the Kindred
Point of Junction.

The First Phase in the demonstration of every Strategetic Proposition is
determined by the following:

THEOREM

*Given the Normal ability to move, to determine the Normal motif and
direction of movement.*

1. Designate that army having the advantage in Time and express such
advantage by the symbol +T, express the corresponding disadvantage in Time
which appertains to the opposing army, by the symbol -T, and such symbols
will constitute the First Term of the First Phase of the demonstration of any
Prime Strategetic Proposition.

2. Express that superiority, equality, or inferiority in Numbers, which
appertains to each of the opposing armies by the symbols +N, =N,-N,
respectively; and such symbols will constitute the Second Term of the First
Phase of the demonstration of any Prime Strategetic Proposition.

3. Express the objectives designated by the plus terms of the Strategic
Syllogism, viz.:

(a) Objective of +A = Objective Plane, *i.e.*, O.P.

(b)   ”   +S = Logistic Horizon, *i.e.*, L. H.

(c)   ”   +M = Point of Junction, *i.e.*, P. J.

and the symbols denoting such objectives will constitute the Third Term in
the First Phase of the demonstration of any Prime Strategetic Proposition.

4. Combine those three terms which appertain to the advantage in Time, then combine those three terms which appertain to the disadvantage in Time, and the resulting equation when expanded will depict:

(a) The normal ability to move.

(b) The normal motif of movement.

(c) The normal directions of movement which appertain to each of the opposing armies.

EXAMPLE

White. $(+T+N) + (+A+S+M)$

Black. $(-T-N)\ \ + (-A-S-M)$

EXPANDED

First Term.	$+T$	$=$	Normal ability to move.			
Second Term.	$+N$	$=$	Normal motif of movement, (a) Detachments, (b) Exchanges.			
Third Term	$+O.\ P.$	$=$	Normal objective of $+A$.			
	$+L.\ H.$	$=$	"	"	"	$+S$.
	$+P.\ J.$	$=$	"	"	"	$+M$.

Hence, in the foregoing example the normal direction of movement for White may be either toward the Objective Plane with the Column of Attack, or toward the Logistic Horizon, or the Point of Junction with the Column of Support, or toward both objectives, with both columns simultaneously.

Meanwhile, the Black army having the disadvantage in Time is unable to move, and consequently is stationary.

Furthermore, White having the superiority in Numbers may move with an equal force against either objective designated by the Third Term of the equation, and with his excess force against one or more adverse vital points, simultaneously, against which latter movement, Black obviously has no adequate defence.

TACTICO-LOGISTIC INEQUALITY

The Tactico-Logistic Inequality is the algebraic expression of the relative advantages and disadvantages in Time and in Numbers appertaining to opposing Strategetic Entireties.

Such advantages and disadvantages are denoted by the terms, viz.:

+T. Signifies the absolute advantage in Time, *i.e.*, the ability of an army, a grand column, a wing or a corps d'armee to move, while the opposing force must remain stationary.

-T. Signifies the absolute disadvantage in Time, *i.e.*, the obligation of an army, a grand column, a wing, or a corps d'armee to remain stationary, while the opposing force is in motion.

+N. Signifies the absolute advantage in Numbers, *i.e.*, the larger number of corps d'armee.

-N. Signifies the absolute disadvantage in Numbers, *i.e.*, the smaller number of corps d'armee.

=N. Signifies the equality in Numbers, *i.e.*, the same number of corps d'armee.

There are six forms of the Tactico-Logistic Inequality, viz.:

$$1. \ \frac{+T+N}{-T-N}$$

$$2. \ \frac{+T=N}{-T=N}$$

$$3. \ \frac{+T-N}{-T+N}$$

$$4. \ \frac{-T+N}{+T-N}$$

$$5. \ \frac{-T=N}{+T=N}$$

$$6. \ \frac{-T-N}{+T+N}$$

INITIAL STRATEGETIC EQUATION

The Initial Strategetic Equation is made up of those terms which compose the Strategic Syllogism and the Tactico-Logistic Inequality, viz.:

$$\overline{(+A+S+M) + (+T+N)} - \overline{(-A-S-M) + (-T-N)} =$$
the Normal Motif and Direction of Effort.

RULE

1. Set down in parenthesis those terms of the Strategic Syllogism which appertain to White.

Set down in parenthesis those terms of the Tactico-Logistic Inequality which appertain to White.

Connect the two kindred terms thus constructed, by the sign of addition, to show that each is to augment the other, and superscore all by the same vincula to show that all are to be taken together to form one side of the resulting equation.

2. Repeat this process for the Black terms to construct the second side of the Initial Strategetic Equation, and separate the White from the Black terms by a minus sign.

STRATEGETIC VALUES

The Strategetic Values of the terms contained in the Strategic Syllogism and in the Tactico-Logistic Inequality are shown by the appended tables, viz.:

TABLE OF STRATEGIC VALUES.

Term.	Post.	Direction.	Motif.
1. +A	Grand Vertex	Tactical Key of Objective Plane	To give checkmate
2. +M	Point Proximity en command	Point of Junction	To queen a Pawn
3. +A	Major Vertex	1. Grand Vertex 2. Point Aligned 3. Point en Potence	To gain winning Position with Column of Attack
4. +M	Point Proximity en Menace	Point en Command	To gain winning Position with Column of Support

5.	+M	Point Proximity en Presence	Point en Menace	To gain winning Position with Column of Support
6.	+A	Minor Vertex	1. Major Vertex	To gain Superior Position

			2. Point Aligned	with Column of Attack
7.	+S	Point Proximity en Observation	Point en Presence	To gain Superior Position with Column of Support
8.	+S	Point Proximity en Route	Point en Observation	To gain superior Position with Column of Support
9.	+S	Point Proximity Remote	Point en Route	To gain advantage with Column of Support

TABLE OF LOGISTIC VALUES

Term.

1. +T   Unrestricted privilege to move any Piece.
2. +T   Restricted to moving a Sustaining Piece en counter attack.
3. +T   Restricted to moving an aggressive Covering Piece.
4. +T   Restricted to moving a Passive Covering Piece.
5. +T   Restricted to moving a Supporting Piece.
6. +T   Restricted to moving the King out of check.
7. +T   Restricted to moving the King from an untenable Objective Plane.
8. +T   Restricted to moving a Piece to reduce the value of the Kindred King's Logistic Radii.

TABLE OF TACTICAL VALUES

Term.

1. +N   Larger numbers of Grand Corps d'armee of Evolution.
2. +N   Larger numbers of Major Corps d'armee of Evolution.
3. +N   Larger numbers of Minor Corps d'armee of Evolution.
4. +N   Larger numbers of Corps d'armee of Position.

PRIME STRATEGETIC PROPOSITION
SECTION TWO

PRIME STRATEGETIC PROPOSITION
SECTION TWO

THEOREM.

Given any Strategetic Situation to determine the True Tactical Sequence.

DEMONSTRATION.

(*First Phase.*)

Let the term +A in its degree represent the relative advantage in Position of the Column of Attack; +S in its degree the relative advantage in Position of the Column of Support, and +M in its degree the relative advantage in Position of the Column of Manoeuvre; let equality in Position of the several Columns be represented by the terms =A, =S, =M, and let inferiority in Positions of the several Columns be represented by the terms -A, -S, -M, and let those terms appertaining to the White Columns be written above a line and those terms appertaining to the Black Columns be written below the line, and let that collection of terms containing the plus and equal signs of greater Strategetic value be the Major Premise and that collection of terms containing the signs of lesser strategetic value be the Minor Premise of the *Strategic Syllogism* thus constructed.

Let the ability to move while the opposing force must remain stationary be represented by the term +T, and let the converse be represented by the term -T, and let superiority in Numbers be represented by the term +N; the equality in Numbers by the term =N, and inferiority in Numbers by the term -N, and let the combining of any form of the terms T and N constitute a *Tactico- Logistic Inequality.*

Let any combination of that Strategic Syllogism which appertains to a given Strategetic Situation with the corresponding Tactico-Logistic Inequality, form the *Initial Strategetic Equation.*

Let the plus terms and the equality terms, which are contained in the Initial Strategetic Equation, be expanded into their highest forms according to the table of Strategetic Values, and annex to each of such terms that numeral which expresses the relative rank of such term in those calculations which appertain to the pending Prime Strategetic Proposition.

Compare the values so obtained and let the highest *Strategetically* be regarded as the menace most immediately decisive, then:

If the term +T appertain to the Piece operating such menace, let such Piece be regarded as the Corps d'armee en Menace, and the Objective of such menace as the Prime Decisive Point; the occupation of such Point by such Piece as the Normal Motif of Offensive Effort, and the Logistic Radius connecting the Point of Departure occupied by such Piece and the Prime Decisive Point as the Normal Direction of Offensive Effort.

If the term +T does NOT apply to that menace which combined with the term +T would be most immediately decisive, then:

By further comparison of the terms of the Initial Strategetic Equation, select that Decisive Menace strategetically next in sequence to which the term +T does appertain; and let the Piece operating such Decisive Menace be regarded as the Corps d'armee en Menace; the Objective of such menace as the Prime Decisive Point; the occupation of such Point by such Piece as the Normal Motif of Offensive Effort, and the Logistic Radius connecting the Point of Departure occupied by such Piece and the Prime Decisive Points as the Normal direction of Offensive Effort.

Provided:

Whenever the term +T appertains to a Menace not so immediately decisive as another menace operated by an adverse army, column, wing or corps d'armee, but to which the term +T does *not* appertain, then: the Normal motif of Effort is *defensive*, and the Normal direction of Defensive Effort is along the Logistic Radius between the Point of Departure of that Kindred Piece, which by the advantage of the term +A, is able to nullify the adverse most immediately Decisive Menace and that Point of Command which is the Objective of such Effort en Defence and from whence such adverse most immediately Decisive Menace may be nullified.

The second or Intermediate Phase of the Prime Strategetic Proposition appertains to Grand Manoeuvres; and the third, or Final Phase, appertains to Grand Operations.

However vast one's capabilities may be, there is no mind so comprehensive but that it has much to learn from other minds which have preceded it, and no talent is so potential but that its development is proportional to its exercise.

For no matter how broad and exact one's knowledge, the application of such knowledge alone constitutes Art, and the value of such knowledge always is commensurate to the degree of skill attained in the use of it.

Hence, there is a training of the physical senses which gives quickness and strength to the eye, the ear and the hand; a training of the nervous organism which gives courage to the heart, clearness to the brain, and steadiness to the body; a training of the intellect which fructifies in originality, ingenuity, profundity and exactness of calculation.

Such training is to be acquired only from systematic study of the best productions by Masters of the Art, and by incessant practice with the best proficients.

www.ingramcontent.com/pod-product-compliance
Lightning Source LLC
Chambersburg PA
CBHW021233020726
47498CB00008B/2821